The Phantom Limbs of the Rollow Sisters

The Phantom Limbs of the Rollow Sisters

Timothy Schaffert

BLUEHEN BOOKS
A MEMBER OF
PENGUIN PUTNAM INC.
NEW YORK

This is a work of fiction. Names, characters, places, and incidents either are the product of the author's imagination or are used fictitiously, and any resemblance to actual persons, living or dead, business establishments, events, or locales is entirely coincidental.

BlueHen Books
a member of
Penguin Putnam Inc.
375 Hudson Street
New York, NY 10014

Library of Congress Cataloging-in-Publication Data

Schaffert, Timothy.
The phantom limbs of the Rollow sisters / Timothy Schaffert.
p. cm.
ISBN 0-399-14900-7
1. Women—Nebraska—Fiction. 2. Antique dealers—Fiction. 3. Nebraska—Fiction. 4. Sisters—Fiction. I. Title.
PS3619.C325 P47 2001056587
813'.6—dc21

Printed in the United States of America
10 9 8 7 6 5 4 3 2 1

This book is printed on acid-free paper. ♾

Book design by Marysarah Quinn

I would like to thank the Nebraska Arts Council and the writing program of the University of Nebraska–Lincoln for their great support. I also thank the following people: Rodney Rahl and Maud Casey, and my mentors Judith Slater and Gerald Shapiro, for their generosity as readers and friends; Hilda Raz and *Prairie Schooner;* Elizabeth Taggart, Andy Morkes, and the folks at Ferguson Publishing; Leslie Prisbell and all the good people of *The Reader,* and Alan and Marcia Baer. And so many thanks to Greg Michalson and Alice Tasman for their commitment to this book.

For my parents,
Larry and Donita

The Phantom Limbs of the Rollow Sisters

1.

IN HER SECONDHAND SHOP, MABEL stretched out on the fainting sofa, feeling tipsy from the summer's heat, not knowing, for a moment, if it was June, July, or August. She shook up a leaking snow globe, the white flakes settling in the laps of lovers on a gondola. Mabel had read in a book on antiques that the snow in snow globes was once made of sawed-up bone. Though Mabel was very young, she often pictured her demise, often hovered above her own Valentino-like funeral with women collapsing and broad-chested men singing impromptu bass tremolo. She'd like to donate her skeleton to a snow globe maker, liked thinking of her remains forever drifting among the plastic landscapes of a souvenir.

Mabel watched her sister Lily put on lipstick in front of the mirror of the decades-old nickel gum machine. Sometimes Mabel wondered if she'd been separated at birth from her *real* sister, for Lily and Mabel shared no resemblance. In a fairy tale, Lily would have been the fair sister of goodness, goldilocked and rosy-faced, and Mabel the nasty one, made up of pointy bones and thin skin and a hank of black hair.

Lily wore only a thrift-shop bra, a pair of jeans, and thick glasses, without which she was only a few blurs from complete lack of sight. After one last drag from her Virginia Slim, she ground the cigarette out in the palm of a mannequin's severed hand.

"I don't know how you can smoke in this heat, Lily," Mabel said. "Everyone's quitting." It had been a terrible summer, and the heat had killed a fifteen-year-old boy in the fields; he dropped dead from a heart attack at eight in the morning cutting tassels from the corn for five bucks an hour. The black-eyed susan by the railroad tracks had blazed yellow for only a week before burning up from the sun. There had never been a better summer for running away to someplace temperate, Mabel thought, fanning herself with an old *Omaha World-Herald*—TWISTER KILLS FIVE—the whirling dust of yellow paper making her sneeze.

Mabel and Lily Rollow lived alone in this junk shop in the country. Tiny hand-painted signs along I-80 directed motorists (ANTIQUES 4 MI., ANTIQUES 3 MI.) onto Highway 34, then off onto gravel roads past a stretch of corn and bean fields and pastures overgrown with tall musk thistle. The gray house stood next to a large, outdated satellite dish in the middle of eighty acres of farm land long left fallow, a few miles from the little nothing town of Bonnevilla (pop. 2,900).

Lily held a tissue to her lips to blot her lipstick. The tissue, marked with the red shape of her kiss, floated softly from the tips of her fingers to the floor. Her boyfriend Jordan had called to say he bought a car and wanted to take her for a ride. At nineteen, he was two years younger than Mabel and a year older than Lily. He was sexy in his tight concert T-shirts and with a clip-on silver hoop over his left eyebrow.

Nights, Jordan came to Lily with gin in the hot months and bourbon in the cold. Even before she noticed his one scarred wrist, Mabel had seen in Jordan an inadequacy for the rough-and-tumble of the world. His breath always smelled of the cheapest wine; Mabel could taste it when she smelled it, a remembered sip stolen as a child at a funeral, and she yearned for its vinegar sting at her throat. Should he ever reopen the wound of his right wrist and this time die, she thought she might fabricate a romance between him and herself and confess it to Lily at the peak of her mourning. Mabel could almost feel that lie waiting in her mouth, hidden beneath her tongue like an unswallowed poison.

"It's not just any car," Lily said. "It's Starkweather's. Sort of. It's not the '49 Ford Charlie owned, but the one he stole from the Lincoln couple he murdered—the '56 Packard." Jordan and Lily were fascinated with the stories of Charlie Starkweather and his fourteen-year-old girlfriend Caril Ann Fugate. Mabel's grandmother had once told of how frightened she'd been those nights on the farm before they caught the killer. Everybody across the state was terrified, she'd said. All the teenagers were afraid to go to drive-ins or out in the country to park and neck. Mabel's grandmother stood those nights at the window hearing thousands of noises coming down along the still and empty country road.

Mabel went to the dilapidated vanity ($75) at the front of the shop to riffle through the mail Lily had tossed unopened across the top of it. There was a letter from their mother who wrote from time to time of broken engagements and new loves. Their mother had left Nebraska more than ten years before, abandoning the girls at their grandmother's second-hand shop then driving southwest, then farther southwest, and farther, until she had tail-spun off the map.

The return address on this letter was new. Their mother's address, though always full of Spanish words, was always in flux. Mabel tore open the envelope, curious to find out if she'd married the old codger who'd made his fortune from selling sea monkeys and trick pepper gum in the pages of comic books. Her mother's life after her father's death had long seemed to have all the romantic posturing of a magazine ad for scotch, all foreign locale and men with gray mustaches whispering into the ears of young ladies. Her mother never wrote much in her letters, but Mabel felt invited to read between the lines for the exotic intrigue and secrets.

Even this month, as Mabel read of nuns and worship, as her mother wrote of being lost then found, Mabel still envisioned lascivious Mexican priests (as beautiful as the young Ricardo Montalban in the old movies Mabel watched during the day) and virgins stuck through with stigmata. "Look," Mabel said, handing Lily the photo from the envelope. In it, their mother knelt at an altar, holding a candle in one hand, cupping its flame with the other, her face only a spot of pale white. *Little lizards*, their mother wrote, *crawl in through the windows sometimes. I throw lit matches at them, hoping they'll leave the way they came in, but they never do. The sisters, though, charm the lizards into a jar and take them out to release them back into the bushes beneath the windows where they live.* In the letter, their mother told of her failed engagement and her new job in a desert vineyard owned by nuns near the border of Arizona. Their mother was still a rather young woman, having had Mabel much too early in her life. Mabel's mother had been only fifteen, her father only eighteen, a couple of brats who thought they were in love for a few minutes. Mabel thought they'd been foolish to try to make a go of it; she would have had an abortion, plain and simple.

Lily held out her hand for the milagro—a tiny iron prayer piece. Their mother had often enclosed milagros through the years, the pieces shaped like body parts, little legs and arms and hands. A heart, a pair of lungs, an eye. *When you have pain*, Mabel's mother had once written, *in your tooth, or your arm, or wherever, you leave the milagro at a site of prayer*. Lily never left the milagros anywhere; she horded them, and she acted like they were meant only for her, something secret shared with her mother. Mabel knew there were no messages for Lily in these tiny pieces of metal, but she was jealous nonetheless. Lily, with her distance and sly half smile and her way of not meeting your eyes, could take anything in hand and grant it mystery. As a little girl, Lily had tormented Mabel by plucking the most meaningless of junk from the antique shop—a bunch of half-broken glass grapes, an ugly, naked porcelain doll, its head a mange of rat-nest human hair—and turning it desirable, making Mabel curse herself for not first recognizing the beauty of the poor, neglected things. Even just a few weeks before, Lily had laid claim to a dilapidated school bus without seats or tires that was parked in the back. Their grandmother had used it as storage, and Lily emptied it of its junk in order to convert it into a private room for the summer. She still kept all her things in her upstairs room, still had to come in to use the bathroom, and still spent most of her early evening hours in the shop next to the window air conditioner, but nights she slept in the bus on a thin mattress draped with mosquito net. Lily called it her apartment, and she had even painted its inner and outer walls pink.

Lily put the milagro in her mouth and knocked it around with her tongue. She looked through all the summery dresses on the rack in the corner, the wire hangers shrieking on the metal rod, and picked out a sleeveless dress with a cherry print. The dress reminded Mabel of the one Marilyn Monroe wore in *The Misfits*. Lily took off her jeans, then stepped into the dress that fit tight and wouldn't zip. *But how pretty she looks*, Mabel thought. Lily wasn't all that fat anymore, but she wasn't thin either, and what fat she had she carried well. Many men liked Lily for her head of curls and her old-style horn-rimmed glasses. Mabel picked up a pliers from a toolbox and went to Lily to fix the stuck zipper.

"How's Jordan able to buy a car, anyway?" Mabel said.

"His dad fired him last week." Jordan's father was the barber in Bonnevilla, and Jordan had done nails, buffing and inching back cuticles and gluing on tiny fancies, at a table in the back of the barbershop. Now Jordan only worked a few nights a week, playing his guitar for tips at the steakhouse in town.

"You'd know just as well as I would," Lily said, pushing aside a collection of scarves to see into a full-length mirror. "Considering you and him have been so chummy lately."

"What do you mean?" Mabel asked.

"You talk to him a lot when I'm not around. I mean, when he comes here, and I'm not here, I know you two talk to each other."

"What are you trying to say, Lily?" Mabel asked, coaxing. She felt a blush hot in her cheeks and throat, anticipating a scuffle. She didn't like arguing. Dispute and confrontation made her throat swell shut and her eyes run. But she felt so much closer to Lily when Lily was provoked. Mabel and Lily were just orphans, really, like *Orphans of the Storm*. In the shop was a box of glass slides for projecting on the screen of movie theaters. Though Mabel had seen only a few of the silent movies featured on these coming-attractions slides, she'd often cast the pictures onto the wall with a flashlight, imagining the stories behind the strange titles: *The Sibyl's Handmaiden; Chinatown Wastrels; The Yellow Piano; The Phantom Limbs of Captain Moore*. The satellite dish in the backyard piped in some old-movie channels that Mabel watched religiously. She most longed to see all the movies of the Gish sisters. She loved the pictures of them holding hands or of them both sweetly gazing upon a common object, their peaked cheeks pressed together, their rouged, puckered lips tiny like black pansies. Why must Lily be so distant? Mabel wondered. Why couldn't we be sisters famous for our devotion?

As Lily spoke, she tied up her curls in a ponytail with a souvenir scarf of the Niagara Falls depicting honeymooners going over in barrels. "What am I *trying* to say?" Lily said. "Well, Mabel, I'm trying to say that when I'm not here, you and Jordan talk. That's what I'm *trying* to say, and I think that's pretty much exactly what I fucking said. What I said is what I'm trying to say. The fucking end. I think a better question would be, What the fuck are you trying to say?"

"You know exactly what I'm trying to say," Mabel said, though not sure herself. She pinched the pliers onto the head of the zipper and gently closed Lily's dress, careful not to catch Lily's soft pink skin in the ragged teeth.

"I don't have the first mother-fucking clue what you're trying to say to me," Lily said. Before Mabel could speak again, Lily continued. "Is what you're trying to say to me that I'm accusing you of trying to steal Jordan away?"

"Yes," Mabel said, looking at Lily's reflection in the mirror. "Yes. That's what we're talking about, isn't it? Why can't you ever just say what's in your head? What are you so afraid's going to happen?"

"Look," Lily said, "you may feel guilty . . . you may have a guilty conscience about the time you spend alone with Jordan, or the feelings you may have for Jordan, but that's your own thing. I'm not accusing you of anything."

There are photographs of us, Mabel thought, evidence of two sorrowful and frightened sisters, and there are notes we wrote to each other. *Complete and utter orphans*, she thought. "Why don't you ever talk to me about things?" Mabel said softly, fussing with the back of Lily's dress, smoothing out a wrinkle. She was so worn out by her own complaint. Lily's absence was an old absence.

"I talk to you," Lily said, walking to the stairs. Her voice built as she went up to her room. "I talk to you all the time. Don't you ever listen?" This was Lily's way of turning everything around, Mabel knew, her way of trying to come across as the one sorely misunderstood.

Mabel thought of a retort, and she ran over to stand at the bottom of the stairs. "Who are you trying to convince, Lily?" she called up. "There's no one here but us." Think of us old, she would have said if Lily hadn't slammed the door. Think of you in your wheelchair and me with a rat on a platter, me all Bette Davis late-career screech.

Mabel picked up a dusty perfume bottle and pinched at the bulb of the atomizer, misting her throat with a fragrance that somehow suggested flappers and Gatsby. The thing was, Mabel hadn't spoken much to Jordan lately or to Lily. She'd been spending most of her hours driving up and down the gravel roads across the state looking for abandoned farmhouses to pillage. Mabel had been running the secondhand store on her own since the day her grandmother packed one shallow suitcase and booked a flight to Orlando, Florida, only a few months before. Her grandmother's sister lived there in a condo in a retirement complex near a beach, along a street called Seashell Circle. "Now that Lily's out of school," her grandmother announced the night of Lily's graduation in June, "you girls can look after yourselves." Though Mabel and Lily were sad to see her go, they were mostly shocked to see her emerge from her room at all, let alone smiling and wearing a brand-new red dress. She also wore a Raquel Welch wig she'd ordered from an ad in a tabloid sometime before but never removed from its box. It was as if the undertaker had crept in with brush and makeup palette to make her grandmother look exactly as she had looked in life. For a long time, Mabel's grandmother had been nothing more than a squeak of the floorboards and a thin stick of light beneath her shut bedroom door.

So Mabel took to the roads and salvaged anything she could from the old places, finding something to steal from even the emptiest of ruins—steam-heat radiators, cement gargoyles, the drawer pulls off built-in wardrobes, antique keys left in old locks. As the banks foreclosed on the area farms, rich people from town, the bankers and lawyers, bought the land for their dream houses and a few horses and maybe a Zen garden of fountains and imported rock. These people liked to fill their new luxury homes with artifacts of old farmhouses. They haunted the junk shop for doors of ornate woodwork or squares of stamped tin or ball-and-claw foot tubs.

Mabel loved her solitary drives across the counties, though all she had was a beaten-down Jimmy that frequently clunked to a complete stop on a back road. Deep in the country there wasn't a junction every mile, and the highways, though marked on a map, were often nothing more than weed-choked paths of broken pavement that dead-ended no place special. In the daytime, Mabel didn't mind the search for help. She'd jump a fence and cross a feedlot to drink from the pipe of a windmill. She'd watch the hawks circle then land in the trees planted for windbreaks at the edges of the fields. She'd eventually scare up a farmer who'd probably make fun of her lack of mechanical know-how, but the mocking was usually playful and flirty and Mabel enjoyed it. The fact was, Mabel had taken a few courses in mechanics from a community college, but she liked getting lost and needing help. She liked kicking up new people from a landscape so forsaken.

With Lily in her bedroom, Mabel returned to the fainting sofa. "Eat me," Mabel mumbled, to Lily maybe or to no one in particular. "Bite me." *You're much too easygoing,* Mabel remembered her mother telling her, back when Mabel's father was still alive. *People will stomp all over you, if you're not careful.* What kind of a thing was that to tell an eight-year-old girl, Mabel now wondered. "Kiss my rosy red," she said. She picked up a fedora from a hat stand, spanked off its dust, and put it on. Size 7 1/8. She felt a static electricity working out from the brim of the hat, lifting strands of hair from her skin. She used to think that snap of shock was her father having become some short-wired ghost, giving her a little smooch. Sometimes Mabel saw her father's reflection in the corners of glass or caught scent of the clove gum he constantly chewed, and she knew he remained watchful and curious about the ways of her life. Mabel wasn't at all religious, but it only made sense that her father kept near. His blood was still inside of her, after all.

Jordan drove up just as all the old clocks for sale on the wall began their fractured chiming. "Anybody got the time?" Jordan said, smirking and stepping in. The shop's light glinted on the key he wore on a shoestring around his neck. Mabel and Lily first met Jordan a year or so before when he'd come out to sell some torn-up Louis L'Amours. Mabel bought everything he brought out over the months. She paid much too much for the metal ribs of an old barrel and the red tailfin of a wrecked '57 Chevy. Jordan's teeth were already yellow and broken from too much nicotine and sugar, so he had a shy, tight-lipped smile Mabel and Lily both fell for.

He leaned over the back of the sofa and Mabel touched at the key swinging from the end of its string. "What's that key to, anyway?" Mabel said.

"Some lock somewhere," Jordan said, shrugging. "But I got this deal I've got to strike up with you. Think you'll buy this?" He held out a silver egg-shaped container, and he twisted off its top to show her the green stains inside. He said, "In this, you'd cure your betel nuts in lime."

"I don't know," Mabel said, suddenly tired of contemplating the price of junk.

Jordan set the betel-nut thing next to Mabel on the sofa, and he shouted out for Lily. He took a swig from a little bottle of Vicks Formula 44 he carried in his pants pocket. "Oh, Lily," he sung out.

He loved Lily very much, Mabel knew, but Lily was devoted to no one in her life. She was only moved by the attention of strangers, particularly strange men in their late twenties, men who maybe had a divorce already, or at least some well-earned disillusion. Lily worked nights at the steakhouse and days at the counter of a bakery in Bonnevilla. The bakery was across the street from a Texaco station and down the street from the police station and the library. Mechanics and cops and mustached librarians in tweed would come in to buy stale pastries at half price and to tease her about the coffee as black and nasty as bilgewater.

It did seem to Mabel, as she watched Lily come down the stairs, that Lily wore their father's suicide almost seductively. Maybe the men sitting alone in the bakery, leaning in toward her as she poured her awful coffee, would smell her perfume, a perfume as uncomplicated, as unoriginal as White Shoulders, and remember some other's throat, some other's wrist. They'd notice her looking vaguely wrecked—her lipstick smeared a little or an earring gone or a button gone from her blouse—and these men would love her for a sadness they hadn't caused.

Lily walked slowly down the stairs having put on a pair of white pumps too long in the toe and too high in the heel. Her dress was unzipped again, and she turned her back to Jordan without a hello. "Do me up, hon," she said, and Jordan obliged, moving in close behind her, putting his lips to the skin of her shoulder as he zipped her dress. He noticed an insect on her neck, and he blew it away before kissing her there. The insect landed on the back of Mabel's hand. It was a strange black ant with wine-colored wings that looked like ornate paper-cuttings. Mabel suspected these odd bugs, these winged ants and white bees she'd been noticing lately, were a result of the new genetically altered crops farmers were resorting to.

Lily winked at Mabel as Jordan kissed her, and she stretched her neck for more of Jordan's affection. "I'm sorry we fought, Mabel," Lily said, nearly whispering. "You're welcome to hate me for the rest of the night, just don't hate me forever." Mabel often daydreamed of hating Lily forever. She wished she could sustain her anger the way Lily did, the way Lily might spend days not speaking because of some slight, shut up in her room with old *Vogues* and a handkerchief wrapped around her hot head as if she were convalescing. Lily had convinced herself that her pain was original, unique, unlike the pain endured by anyone anywhere in the history of time. Over the years, Mabel had tried to teach her otherwise by collecting short articles depicting worse tragedies from the back pages of the newspaper. She'd leave these clippings on Lily's pillow, stories like the one about the girl who pushed her twin down an old well or the one about a woman who slowly poisoned her sister by stirring iron filings into her nightly cup of chamomile.

Lily unrolled the short sleeve of Jordan's shirt to get at the pack there. "This is candy," Lily said.

"Yeah," he said, "I'm trying to quit smoking. But look here," and he took one of the bubble gum cigarettes from the pack and held it to his lips. He blew into it and a dusting of fine, powdery sugar made a cloud. "Just like smoke," he said.

"Where's the car?" Lily said, waving her hand in the air, refusing the bubble gum. Jordan took Lily's wrist, then Mabel's, and led them out to the front porch. Beneath the lamp that lit the gravel drive sat the two-door Packard faded away to a pale gray. Rust spots like gunshot riddled the side of it. A dishtowel hung in place of the glass of one of the side windows.

"One of those ninety-nine-dollar paint jobs and she'll be the prettiest girl on the block," Jordan said. Mabel imagined riding in the back of the car to the river on a muggy afternoon, wearing a swimsuit with a beach towel wrapped around her waist. Jordan would be in a pair of cutoff jeans and a tropical shirt all unbuttoned, Lily beside him painting her toenails with her foot up and pressed against the dashboard. They'd listen to the old records her father had taped—Joe Jackson and Elvis Costello and The Clash.

Jordan took a box from the backseat of the car. "This

woman in town had meant to open up a Starkweather museum. She put a new engine in the car and everything, so people could go for joy rides in it. But she ran out of money." He took from the box the other artifacts he'd bought from the woman: a doll Caril Ann had made from twisting up a Kleenex, and a sign Caril had put up on the door of her house where she and Charlie holed up for six days after he killed her family. The sign read: STAY AWAY EVERY BODY IS SICK WITH THE FLU.

"I'm not buying any of this from you," Mabel said. "It's borderline perverted. Not to mention hexed." But Lily, with reverence, lifted the impossibly fragile Kleenex doll from the box and held it in her palm. She touched a fingertip to its bald head. Lily and Jordan once took a bus to Lincoln to visit Starkweather's grave at the Wyuka Cemetery and to attempt a séance.

"None of this stuff is for sale, anyway," Jordan said. "I robbed that woman blind and this is all going to only appreciate in value." Jordan opened the doors for Lily and Mabel. Mabel slipped into the backseat and sat back. The vinyl was torn, the cushions lumpy, and she wondered if there might be something grisly sewn into the seat—the silent remains of something unspeakable. Jordan didn't start the car yet, savoring it, holding the steering wheel, steering a little, fiddling with the radio knob and pushing in the cigarette lighter. The car smelled of must and mice. A broken spring in the seat poked at the back of Mabel's leg. It seemed to Mabel that, in such a car, one would be inspired by the spirit of renegade youth and not be scared of anything. But the only thing that affected Mabel was the view out the window. The sun was setting at the edge of the desolation, casting its sharp glow across the miles of nothingness to be traveled before reaching a good place.

Mabel longed for the circle of lights of the Ferris wheel at the fairgrounds on the edge of town. The Hamilton County fair had just ended after a long weekend; as a little girl, Mabel had sat on the roof of the porch to watch the lights of the fair spin and flash, the carnival like a ghost city, a midwestern Brigadoon, rising from the mist once a year. On still nights she could hear the smash of the demolition derby or even the bleat of sheep penned and judged. Even years later, walking alongside the booths and tents and trucks of the carnival, the air thick with humidity and the smell of cotton candy and candied apples, Mabel wouldn't have been surprised to see her father holding Lily up to pick a rubber duck from a tub of running water. On the bottom of the duck would be the number of Lily's prize, a plastic shark's tooth on the end of a necklace that Lily would give to her mother to wear. When her parents fussed over Lily, when Lily was small, was when Mabel most felt part of a family, when Lily's crying and laughing, napping and waking, were of great amusement and concern. Mabel would never forget sitting on her mother's lap in the old apartment one Sunday, both of them rapt and silent watching Lily sleep naked but for a diaper against her sleeping father's naked chest. Her father lay back on the sofa, Lily in his arms, the funnies spread out on the floor beside them. The Silly Putty they'd been playing with still held the stretched-out image of Dick Tracy's daughter-in-law Moonbeam. "Aren't we lucky?" Mabel's mother whispered in her ear.

At the fair just the night before, Jordan, even three sheets to the wind, had won Lily one of those square, painted mirrors, by knocking over milk bottles with a wrecked baseball, its stitching in pieces. On the mirror was a retro cartoon of R. Crumb's bald-headed *Keep On Truckin'* high-steppers. But Jordan let Mabel have the mirror when Lily disappeared with a gangly, nothing-to-lose carny who felt her up beneath the bleachers of the rodeo. Lily confessed in the middle of the night, in the middle of the midway noisy with heavy-metal music blaring from the Wild Octopus and the Screaming Mimi, and Jordan forgave her because she was in tears—the carny had stolen her ruby earrings by expertly nibbling on her lobes.

"There's a State Highway 666," Jordan said, the car still and silent, "goes south down Arizona. Can you imagine? Driving Starkweather's car down Highway 666?"

The sleeves of Jordan's shirt were too short for his long arms. Lily traced her finger along the scar across Jordan's right wrist. "When you did this," she said to Jordan, "did you leave some kind of note?" *Lily and I wonder about so many of the same things*, Mabel thought, pleased.

In all the months Mabel and Lily had known Jordan, they'd not spoken of his most obvious relation to their father. But the similarity wasn't all that obvious. After all, she thought, their father had succeeded at suicide and Jordan had failed—two very, very different situations.

Mabel listened closely to Jordan's hindered breathing, the old-man's rattle of congestion in his young-man's chest. He was only a boy, just barely nineteen, yet afflicted with a litany of minor ailments and an addiction to over-the-counter remedies. He licked at those cold-medicine lollipops for kids even when he had no sniffle; he constantly popped Advil, sucking the sweet, candy-like coating off each tablet. As he took another hit off his Primatene Mist, Mabel wondered how Lily could just sit there resisting holding his stuffed-up head to her bosom to smooth down his rooster tail and whisper love and comfort.

Jordan recited from his suicide note. *"Think this not,"* he mumbled, *"a tragedy of great proportion. Think it only the delicate misstep of someone's dying life."*

"Hmmmm," Lily hummed, her voice a sexy wink. "You're a poet, sweetie." But Mabel leaned back disappointed. She'd hoped for a letter violent with accusation and spite. These were not the true words of a young man longing for death, and Mabel knew something of fake suicide notes. Before her mother left for Mexico, she took Mabel and Lily aside. "Girls," she'd said, for Mabel and Lily were just very small girls then, Mabel only about ten years old, "I have something for you." She took a piece of paper from her pocket and unfolded it. Mabel recognized her mother's stationery—powder blue with gray kittens next to *Fiona B. Rollow* at the top of the page—and her mother's handwriting, all petite curlicue and extra flourish. But her mother said, "Your father left this note behind. *To whom it may concern,*" she read aloud, "*Please, no one take responsibility for my pain . . . it is my own fault, my own failing. My daughters, please don't blame your mother for my death, and don't blame your mother if she can't take care of you on her own. It would be much too hard for her, as it would be for anyone. I realize what I am about to do is so unfair. But I dug a hole for myself, and I can't get out of it. Sincerely, Eddy Rollow.*"

Mabel had wanted to believe those were her father's words, but it had been impossible. *My daughters? as it would be for anyone? I dug a hole?* It had depressed Mabel even then that her mother wouldn't have known better, wouldn't have known that Mabel and Lily loved their father so much because he was not a man who would write with such formality and stiffness. If Eddy Rollow had left a suicide note, Mabel thought, it would have been in the margins of a favorite book. Or he would have written it on the wall of the kitchenette of the old apartment, his script flowing around the pomegranates and grapes and almonds in the wallpaper's print. Or, more likely, he would have written his words in the dissolving steam of the bathroom mirror.

Now the note, which Mabel kept in a fire-safe box, was taking on the qualities of age and of damage from the constant opening and closing. Each time Mabel took the note out to read it again, its folds crumbled and tore a bit more, and more of the words, in pencil, had begun to fade away into the powder blue. Always before, Mabel had hated the letter, this evidence of her mother's deception, but she'd grown to need it. As its words dissolved and the paper fell apart, as it slowly ceased to exist, it became something true. This lie became an honest portrait of Mabel's mother and her confusion.

If Mabel had been in the front seat with Jordan, she would have taken his hand and kissed his scar, then held his hand to her cheek. She and Lily knew none of the details of their father's suicide, except that it involved a gun. They didn't know if he'd put it in his mouth or in his ear, didn't know if it had taken apart his head or had left a simple clean hole. Mabel had even fantasized that he'd merely meant to shoot himself in the foot, to injure himself to get disability. He'd often complained of his job as a foreman at a company that manufactured trailer homes. Mabel had loved how his skin smelled of the sawdust from freshly cut wood, and she'd sit on his lap and nuzzle her nose in his neck as he read from the funnies page at night. He particularly enjoyed Andy Capp, so much so that he even ate a bag of Andy Capp–brand Hot Fries every day from the lunchroom vending machine.

Mabel touched at the back of Jordan's neck; his skin was hot, almost feverish, and damp with sweat. "Drive us someplace," she said, looking toward the little yellow lights of Bonnevilla. Mabel wished Jordan would drive them quickly away, fast enough for them to move ahead in time, for her to look back on the whole of her life and learn something about who she would become. Would she have any babies, and would she be the type of mother to abandon them, or would she be the type of mother to steal them away and vanish without a trace? Actually, she couldn't see herself with children at all—she imagined something of a monastic life for herself, imagined a life of stomped grapes and kept bees and scratchy robes with belts of rope.

2.

STREET LAMPS LIT THE EMPTY SIDEwalks of the town square. The only places still open were the steakhouse and a pool hall that Mabel hadn't been in since she was four years old. As they passed, Mabel could remember the smell of her dad's Old Golds doused out in mugs of flat beer. Mabel had felt like a celebrity as she'd spun around on the stool, gathering up the attention of all the barflies and pool players. She once ordered a Shirley Temple because that was what she'd heard a little girl in a beret on TV order in a hotel lounge, but her father had said with a wink, "Nah, give her something stronger, Les. Mix her up a Roy Rogers."

As Jordan parked the car in front of The Red Opera House, Mabel said, "What would I have been doing in the pool hall at four years old? And where were you, Lily?"

"Mom needed a break from having a rowdy four-year-old

all day long," Lily said. "And I would have been practically a baby, so he couldn't have taken me to the bar." She added, "I would've been just about a year old," pleased with her youth. "It would have been so inappropriate."

"One foot in the womb," Jordan said, pinching Lily's baby-fat cheek.

Mabel's father quit drinking shortly after that night he treated her to a Roy Rogers. Mabel reached over and combed her fingers through Lily's ponytail, pitying her because she never got to have a mocktail with their daddy.

"I found a way to break into The Red Opera House," Jordan said, looking into the rearview at Mabel. Mabel had longed for years to get inside. She'd heard of the curtain hand-painted with birds by a Dutch artist and of ruby-eyed dragonflies in the stained-glass chandeliers. "There are murals on the wall of people in masks," Jordan said, telling her about how he'd found his way inside only a few nights before.

Lily threw open the car door, got out, and kicked off her too-big shoes. She carried one shoe in each hand as she stormed down the sidewalk, away from the opera house. "Lily!" Jordan called. "Lily! Where are you going? What are you mad about?" But Mabel knew this was another of Lily's fits—Lily didn't like Mabel and Jordan's shared interest in junk and old buildings. Mabel knew that Lily was headed toward the end of the block lit up by Jordan's father's barbershop; it was after hours, but Mr. Swain often spent evenings in his barber chair avoiding Mrs. Swain at home. Mrs. Swain, when stewed, which was often, became a comic-strip domestic situation, her brittle bleached hair up in rollers, her housecoat hanging open over a flimsy slip, a rolling pin a weapon in her hand. So Mr. Swain kept a VCR at the barbershop, along with his collection of old Suzanne Pleshette movies and the complete episodes of *The Bob Newhart Show*. He'd watch the tapes on his black-and-white portable, drinking Windsor and smoking Swisher Sweets. Both Lily and Mabel had terrible crushes on Mr. Swain; he, like their own parents, had been only a teenager when he'd fathered Jordan, so he was an extravagantly young older man with thick yellow hair and a flat stomach. He cut hair in his Levis and tight, white T-shirt and wore a plastic comb tucked behind his ear. Lily claimed to Mabel that he once unbuttoned his jeans and pushed them down a bit for her to see a horned red devil with "The Devil Made Me Do It!" tattooed at his lower abdomen.

"Just forget about Lily," Mabel said, though she knew Jordan could never. He didn't even hear Mabel say it; he was concentrating on the sight of Lily walking away.

In the stone at the top of the building before them was written "The Red Opera House 1893," but the bricks had been painted green for as long as Mabel could remember. Mabel wondered if "red opera" referred to the kinds of productions the theater had staged—bloody conflagrations in all red costume against red backdrops, the actors wailing and moaning their music as they fell to the floor stabbed or shot through.

Jordan got out and held his hand into the backseat to help

Mabel from the car. Though he moved toward the alley, he didn't take his eyes from Lily's back. But once off the street, he cheered up, and he nonchalantly pushed open a hinged basement window with the toe of his boot. After crawling in through the basement, Jordan and Mabel walked up into the grocery store. Jordan climbed onto a corner pinball machine to pull a ladder down from a door in the ceiling, and he and Mabel both stepped up into the opera house of the second floor.

Mabel was anxious to see the walls and the stage of the theater lit by the full moon, but she couldn't take her eyes off Jordan pushing aside a cobweb to clear Mabel's path, a web so thick it looked like a nylon stocking. "No one's spoken a word here for years," Mabel whispered in Jordan's ear, thinking of Mary and Dickon and their secret garden. The room was surprisingly cool, and she thought she could hear the drip of a faucet. A painted Ophelia, in a dress with the iridescence of peacock feathers, drowned on the door to the dressing rooms. Lady Godiva with butterflies in her long tresses rode a horse across the ceiling.

"It's so beautiful in here," Mabel said, touching the burned wick of a candle on a chandelier that sat in a heap in the corner. "Why don't they let anyone up to see it?"

"The place is falling apart," Jordan said, "and it would be too expensive to repair. All the boards are rotten through. We could fall through the floor at any given minute. So walk on your tiptoes and keep yourself as light as you can." Jordan opened the doors to a wardrobe, and the glassy eyes of a fox stole caught a sliver of moonlight and stared back at them.

"I'm taking Lily to Mexico," Jordan said. He blurted it, like he'd been waiting and waiting for just the right moment but had given up.

"The beer tastes like skunk down there," was all Mabel could think of to say. "You have to put fruit in it to drink it." For years, Mabel's mother had discouraged Mabel and Lily from visiting her, painting a portrait of Mexico as a place of banditry and bad water, a place where children lost their arms in factory machines and dead hookers were left to rot in the streets. Even when very young, Mabel had seen through her mother's efforts to disguise her new home as uninhabitable, but Mabel had also grown comfortable with the idea of her mother as virtually unreachable in her foreign land. It was one thing Mabel had been able to rely upon—her mother in a place that children would not want to be, a place where black widows lay eggs in your ear canal and snakes slept curled-up in your cowboy boots.

"I read in the newspaper," Mabel said, "about a pregnant woman in Mexico whose sister drugged her, induced labor, sold the baby, then told her sister the child had died." Mabel had clipped the article and held onto it, saving it to put on Lily's pillowcase when she had her next long fit.

"It's time Lily saw her mother again," Jordan said with a shrug, as if saying, *Isn't it obvious?* As if saying, *Don't we want the best for Lily?*

Mabel walked away from Jordan and looked out a broken window, down to the familiar street. The streets of the town square were all brick with patches of gray concrete. She could hear the rattle and bump of every car she'd ever ridden in as it crossed the streets, could feel the rough ride in her spine. If Jordan took Lily away, even for just a week, even if they never made it to Mexico, everything would change for all of them.

Jordan took Mabel's hand, and he slipped a ring onto her finger. In the set of the ring was an opaque sphere, and Jordan flipped it open on its tiny hinges to show something could be kept inside. "I found it under the stage," he said. "There's all kinds of things under there. Maybe it was good luck for the actors to drop things through the loose floorboards or something." Jordan lit his cigarette lighter, led the way to the base of the stage, and pushed aside a panel. The stage was so low to the floor that Mabel had to lower herself to her stomach to get beneath.

As she bellied her way across the floor, she could hear Jordan crawling in behind her. Her sandal fell off, and she felt Jordan touch the sole of her bare foot. She felt his fingertips stepping as light as spider's legs across her heel and up along her ankle. She remembered the afternoon that her mother read aloud her father's unlikely suicide note and how her mother then took Mabel and Lily to the river for a swim. Naked in the cold river water, the three of them hid beneath the trestle as a train crossed. They shivered and held each other. Unable to hear anything other than the passing train, they sent wordless messages, Mabel pressing her palm to her mother's stomach, Lily putting her cheek to her mother's breast, her mother running her fingers over the goose bumps of their skin.

Jordan, his face next to Mabel's, relit the lighter, and Mabel leaned back from the heat in her face. "You're filthy," she said, pressing her thumb against a spot of dirt on his cheek. As the lighter went out, Mabel lay back and thought more about her father's last words—he would have written them on thin pieces of paper and baked them into fortune cookies. With a puddle jumper, he'd have smoked the words across the clouds. *You'll live happily ever after*, he would have promised them all.

Jordan tried to find Mabel's lips in the dark, kissing her cheek, then her nose, then her lips. He kissed her only once, then crawled away and back to the front of the stage. With the kiss, Mabel forgave him everything—for liking Lily more and for buying a car to take Lily away. And she forgave him all further destruction; she would forgive him if he ruined Lily and if he ruined her and if he became someone she and Lily could only talk about very carefully.

3.

IT WAS MABEL'S BIRTHDAY, AND LILY had slipped a card beneath her bedroom door, inviting her down to her school-bus apartment for cocktails and cake. As the sun set, Lily unplugged the lava lamp from the thick orange extension chord that snaked in through a break in a window of the bus; in its place, she plugged in a string of blinking Christmas lights. The cord, its other end plugged into an outlet in what had once been a hog shed, into what had once powered a low electrical fence that Lily had once tripped over, jolting her knees, was her only source of electricity.

With the summer so hot, Lily spent only nights on the mattress in the bus, mosquito netting delicately draped above her.

Lily hadn't spoken much to Mabel since the evening a few nights before at The Red Opera House, though she knew she was wrong to be angry. It shouldn't matter that she and Mabel didn't share every interest. Lily should love that Mabel and Jordan were close and could appreciate together the dirty dark recesses of collapsing rooms and the studied appraisal of the worthless. It was sweet, after all, to see them stumble up from that basement window, happy with the precious junk they'd discovered. Lily used to love the antique shop, but after living there for several years, she had become tired of all the topsy-turvy: the old incomplete sets of encyclopedias in the kitchen cabinets; the dishes and saucers on the bookshelves; the chairs and rugs stuffed into the rafters of the ceiling; stamped tin from ceilings rusting in a pile on the floor.

Lily longed to be more peaceable, to remain aloof and serene in the face of her frustrations. She longed to be calm and wise and forgiving. People love you more when you're quiet, Lily imagined, when you can simply accept. When again she saw her mother, Lily would be the sweet, understanding girl that she had never been before, and she and her mother could enjoy an uneventful afternoon of simple questions and simple answers. Aside from some kisses and some hugging when they first saw each other, their reunion would lack all drama. It would lack all punishment. Lily relaxed, imagining the few hours she would spend drinking tea within the mud walls of her mother's cool, blue house. Her mother had written of the papery sound of scorpions on the floor, a sound she said would be soothing if it weren't for the fear of the sting.

Lily had found a traveling cocktail set on a back shelf of

the shop, the worn leather strap of the case having turned as fragile as cardboard. As she assembled the martini glasses, screwing the glass cups into the red metal stems, she decided it would be a perfect evening. Just the night before, as she and Jordan sat naked in the heat of the bus, too hot to touch, Jordan had suggested they go find Lily's mother, that they drive down to the border town where her mother wrote lovely letters to her daughters.

Their mother had called from time to time when Lily and Mabel were still girls. Her voice buzzed and popped with distant noise and tickled Lily's ear. Lily always asked, "What have you been doing?" and her mother always said, "Oh, keeping the wolves at bay." Lily hadn't known what that meant, but she had liked the idea of her mother keeping wolves. She could imagine her in a bungalow along the coast of Mexico, the walls reflecting waves of blue as she licked an oyster from a shell. Near the window overlooking the bay, dirty wolves wrestled. "Can we come to Mexico?" Lily once asked. "Oh, you wouldn't like it here," her mother said. "There are bandits to steal your purse. Black widows build webs above your bed. In the cafés, you can't even get a glass of ice with your pop." At the time, Lily longed for this terrible place as her mother described it. There, she and Mabel and their mother could live in fear and disgust, never answering the knocks at their door because, in a foreign land, no one could be trusted.

Lily put on a dark-blue sleeveless velveteen dress that was too hot for summer but too cool for winter, and she curled the ends of her hair with a disposable butane curling iron she bought at the Everything for a Buck. She and Mabel always dressed up on their birthdays, and they always gave each other gifts. They didn't allow each other to spend a dime, however; they were to find something appropriate in the shop and wrap it up. Lily cheated a bit this year, having gone through a trunk of her father's things in one of the spare rooms. She selected for Mabel a Joan Armatrading album with her father's handwriting on the back of the cover, in the upper corner: BOUGHT OCTOBER 12, 1977, FROM THE LICORICE PIZZA, OMAHA. HAD LUNCH AT THE JOE TESS CAFÉ—FRIED RAINBOW TROUT ON A SLICE OF RYE.

Lily loved having found the record hidden at the bottom of a box of patched-up work jeans. Growing up, she and Mabel had listened over and over to their father's favorite music. They would set a portable record player in the window of Mabel's room and crawl out onto the roof where Lily would smear coconut-scented lotion on Mabel's freckled back and Mabel would soak Lily's hair with spray-on Sun-In. Hours later, Lily would crawl back into the house as a strawberry blonde. With lines of sunburn crossing their shoulders and hips, they walked downstairs to stand in front of the window air conditioner, both exhausted from their afternoon naps. Eventually they learned all the words to all the songs of ELO and Rickie Lee Jones and Roxy Music, all performers their classmates had never even heard of. Especially on summer days, whenever their father's music played, Lily and Mabel adored each other, became Daddy's precious girls, sun-kissed and sweetly sick from the overplaying of Todd Rundgren songs. They glossed their lips and saw themselves as tragically lost to the world. As Lily would drift off to sleep, she'd hear messages from her father in the songs, in the phrases she'd catch in bits and pieces in her drowsiness. Her father existed now to whisper promises in her ear.

As each year passed, Lily's memories of her parents inched a little closer toward the romantically impossible, and Lily had imagined herself a bit more like a character in one of the young-adult paperbacks the girls at school passed around. In these, girls suffered family tragedies or drank too much, or they smoked dope or feared pregnancy. For a few years, Lily had read and reread the battered *Summer, Finally,* about a sixteen-year-old named Summer having an affair with one of her father's friends in the summertime. Lily kept the book hidden in her locker, certain passages marked in the margins by an X in fingernail polish, and the very idea of it all made Lily feel happily trashy and perverse. She had even jotted in her notebook the name of a boy who had signed her father's high school yearbook ("Always stay the same! And shave that silly peach fuzz off your lip!"), Bart Youngblood, a name perfectly and creepily suited for her first-love statutory-rape fantasies. She would fall asleep with thoughts of resting her cheek on Bart's naked chest.

Lily unfolded a card table and chairs and set them in the center of her bus's living room. She'd brought a cake home from the bakery where she worked, and she put it atop the table along with the wrapped Joan Armatrading record, some lilacs tucked into the ribbon's knot. It was night now, the bus lit only by the Christmas lights and a row of candles on the dashboard. She sat down and plucked a candy rose from beneath Mabel's name in blue and broke off its petals. She let each petal melt on her tongue as she tried to imagine what her mother would be like. Because her mother was so young when she had her babies, she would still be only thirty-five now. She could still very well be confused and afraid over all that had fallen apart in the past. Though Lily couldn't yet understand how her mother, how any mother, could have left her girls and never returned, Lily would be generous and patient. For once, Lily would be the mothering soul. Lily's questions would be gentle. *What songs make you think of him? Are there songs that make you think of us?*

She looked up to the house, to the front room, where Mabel stood behind Jordan, her arms around his shoulders. Mabel looked at their reflection in the glass so that she could knot Jordan's tie. Lily wasn't jealous, she reminded herself. There was no jealousy. In only a few days, Lily was certain, Jordan would ask again, as he so often did, if she'd marry him, and this time Lily would say yes. Lily would be engaged when she met her mother again, as well as enrolled in community college. She had signed up only for a watercolor class as of yet, but her mother didn't have to know that. As far as her mother would be concerned, Lily was poised to make none of the mistakes she had.

But as Lily looked at Jordan in the window, this boy too inept to know his own way around a necktie, she wondered how long their approaching marriage would last. And when they divorced, where would she go? Would she find herself flung far, like her mother? Lily imagined herself in some place like Atlantic City, lonely and hopeful, feeling her stomach sink every time the seat of the Ferris wheel dipped down toward the ocean.

Lily's mother had left Lily's father many times in the years before he killed himself. Though Lily always missed her father during the days they spent in their grandmother's house, there in the antique shop, she thrived on her mother's guilt. Lily's mother, frightened of ruining the lives of her children, lavished attention on her daughters during those days of separation. She'd let Lily join her in her bubble bath and even allowed her sips of the peach Riunite she drank from a wide-mouthed water goblet. Her mother had looked so pretty, pink and naked, her wet curls clinging to her cheeks. She'd tickle Lily's ribs with her toes beneath the water.

One afternoon, their mother spirited Lily and Mabel off to Omaha for shopping in an overpriced downtown department store, then lunch at King Fong's Café. Mabel and their mother had chow mein, and Lily, put off by the foreign words on the menu, had a hamburger. After eating, their mother broke open a fortune cookie.

"*Good news will be brought to you by mail,*" she had read, brushing the cookie crumbs from the rabbit fur of her winter coat's lapel. Lily could still remember the café, though she'd never been there since. She remembered the long walk up steep stairs and picking at the pearl in the inlay of the wood tabletop. The dark, ornate chandeliers, with their silhouettes of rolling dragons and black orchids, looked too heavy to be held up by the ceiling. Lily remembered the cold, white sky bright in the cross-shaped windows. There'd been some stained glass in the panes, reminding Lily of church.

"It will be a love letter from Daddy," Mabel told Lily, treating Lily like she was an infant needing consoling and assurance. Lily wanted to sock Mabel in the jaw for it.

"No," Lily's mother said. She started to cry and she pressed a paper napkin to her cheek. "No love letters. He doesn't love me. Why should he love me? Would you?" Lily never knew what to do when her mother cried, when she asked the questions that made no sense, so she did what she always did, which was to look down and wait for Mabel to do something. Mabel finally reached across the table and gently stroked the rabbit fur. "I wish I wouldn't cry in front of my children," her mother said, trying to smile.

Lily wished she wouldn't either. No matter how often her mother cried, Lily never got used to it. When her mother would fall apart, and her mother might fall apart in the middle of anything, Lily couldn't breathe and couldn't think. Sometimes Lily would start crying too, and sometimes that worked to make her mother stop.

At that lunch at King Fong's that day, all three of them sat there distraught, their cosmetics-counter makeovers streaming down their faces, staining the collars of their new blouses. As Lily looked down at her hands and her chewed nails, she saw the price tag still dangling from the cuff.

Good news actually did arrive by mail a few days later, just as the fortune cookie predicted. They'd entered a raffle at the department store and each of them had won a free set-and-style from the hair salon at the back of the store, and the pink coupons featuring a cartoon lady in ridiculously big curlers came to their grandmother's house in a pink envelope. By that time, however, they'd moved back into the apartment in town, and they actually stayed with their father through the rest of that winter and most of that summer and never made it back to that department store. It had relieved Lily to watch the coupons over the months fade and curl in the sun on the windowsill above the kitchen sink.

JORDAN, in a dark blue suit with baggy trousers, his hand-painted tie depicting long-legged women in polka-dot bathing suits, brought down a bucket of ice and a bottle of whiskey for the Manhattans. In his back pocket, he carried a bottle of apple cider. Jordan liked all the sweet drinks, all the coolers flavored like soda pop, and the ices with pieces of fruit. But Lily thought booze should taste like dirt and smoke and wood, and she preferred bourbon or a dark beer.

"When 'arf of your bullets fly wide in the ditch," Jordan quoted from somewhere, examining the portable martini glass, *"don't call your martini a cross-eyed old bitch."*

Mabel carried the sweet vermouth. She looked pretty but too thin in a clingy dress that changed colors from blue to green to purple as she moved in the candlelight. When their mother abandoned them with their lazy grandmother, all the farmers' wives and widows in the area left recipes to encourage their grandmother to cook, to fatten Mabel up. When looking at the yellowed recipe cards, Lily had dreamed of life in their warm little homes, of pictures of Jesus on the walls and the smell of cinnamon and clove in the kitchens.

Mabel put the bottle on the table and opened her other hand to let five chokecherries roll out. A tree on the other side of a fence down the hill dropped the fruit onto their land every late summer. "I didn't have any maraschinos," Mabel said.

Lily ate the sour chokecherry from around its tiny pit, and with the sharp taste she saw her father standing in the pasture, tearing his jeans on barbed wire, the muscles in his arms straining as he reached up to pull down a branch. Even with the branch bent, Lily still couldn't reach the chokecherries, and he'd shake the branch, and she'd try to catch them as they rained in front of her. Because of the sandburs that stuck in Lily's socks, her father would carry her back across the pasture. She'd lay her head on his shoulder and press her lips against his neck, touching her tongue to the salt of his sweat.

"Do you think our mother knows?" Lily said, dropping a chokecherry into the Manhattan that Jordan shook together for her. "About why Daddy did it?" It was a question Lily and Mabel had passed back and forth between each other for years, a question worked smooth like sea glass.

Mom must know something was Mabel's usual answer, but tonight she simply said, "No." Mabel took a ribbon of frosting from the cake and ate it, then sipped her Manhattan, cringing from the bite of the whiskey. "What could she know, really?"

"Seems to me," Lily said, "she'd have some thoughts."

"He had children too young," Mabel said. "Married too young. He was as young as you are now."

"This isn't so young," Lily said, though she couldn't imagine having a baby to look after. She could still remember taking baths in the kitchen sink, her mother washing her hair with a bar of soap. Her own childhood was still fresh in her mind. "How old were you that one birthday?"

"Eight," Mabel said, knowing exactly what Lily was talking about.

"You ever hear about Mabel's eighth birthday?" Lily asked Jordan, and though he nodded, Lily talked about it anyway. Lily put her bare feet up onto Jordan's knees, and crossed her ankles. "Grandpa had died not too long before, but Grandma still had a bull in the pasture. Daddy had helped her sell it, so he put it into the back of the pickup, and me and Mabel and Mom all crammed into the front with Dad to take it to some farm down the road."

"There were tall railings up the sides of the truck," Mabel said, "and the bull broke through them and ran away." They followed the bull as it ran into town trampling through somebody's backyard tomato plants, disrupting a picnic in a park, tearing down Chinese lanterns and a badminton net. Mabel always denied it, but she had cried as the night dragged on, the bull ruining her birthday. But Lily had loved watching something from her tiny life shake awake the whole sleepy town.

"I forget how you caught him," Jordan said.

"We forget too," Lily said. "We think we may have lost him somewhere." It tired her to fill in all the details. She liked how she could just merely suggest something to Mabel, and she could watch the recognition in her face. There hadn't been much of anything that they hadn't seen together.

Lily reached over and tugged a bit on the sleeve of Jordan's suit coat, covering his wrist. She'd have to do something about that scar if she was going to show him off to her mother. "I need to find that last letter Mom wrote to us," Lily said.

Mabel just looked at Lily over the top of the Manhattan she only barely sipped. "Why?" she finally said.

"I need the return address." Lily was tempted to invite Mabel along on her journey, but she knew better. Mabel, her mother, everyone, needed to understand that Lily needed no mothering. They would all see that, in spite of everything, Lily had turned out a good, capable person.

"I was just reading in the paper," Mabel said, "of a woman in Mexico bitten by a brown recluse spider. They had to cut off her arms and her legs and part of her nose."

Lily straightened up in her chair, ready to tell Mabel of her plans. "Mabel . . ." she started, pushing her glasses down on her nose so that everything blurred. She nervously pulled at a loose string at the hem of her dress. "Mabel."

"I already know that you're going to see her," Mabel said. "If that's what you're about to tell me. Jordan told me already. About the two of you going to find Mom."

Lily pushed her glasses back up to see Mabel scowling and concentrating on picking her chokecherry from where it had sunk to the bottom of her Manhattan. Lily looked over at Jordan who couldn't even meet her eyes; he fussed with the end of his necktie. The cool demeanor Lily had practiced all afternoon turned into a migraine headache and tiny bolts of colored light in the corners of her vision. Was everything intimate just gossip to him? He wanted Mabel's attention too much of the time, and it was beginning to make Lily too sick of it all. "Fuck you," Lily said, lifting her feet to kick Jordan's knee. "I could fucking beat the crap out of you," giving him a whack at the side of his head with her open palm.

"Could you not," Jordan said, drowsy-sounding, cringing, "not, you know, slug me?"

"Jordan," Mabel said. "Maybe you should leave us alone for a few minutes."

"Fuck off, Mabel," Lily said. "He's my boyfriend, I'll tell him when he stays and when he goes, all right?"

Jordan started, "I should just tell you . . ."

"Oh, just get the fuck out of here, Jordan," Lily said. "I mean, I have so fucking had it with you right now." She immediately regretted having said it, and she stumbled over the last few words of her outburst. *Tranquility*, Lily thought, hearing the useless recitation she had found in some self-help paperback someone had left behind in the bakery. *Peacefulness. Serenity*.

As Jordan stood, shaky as if on new legs, Lily wanted to

grab the lapel of his pathetic suit and demand that he ignore her and her fits.

"If you'll excuse me, Birthday Girl," Jordan said, brushing his fingers against the cheek of the always-quiet, always-collected Mabel. The whole bus creaked as Jordan headed toward the door, the slow tap of the high heels of his fake-alligator cowboy boots echoing. Lily lowered her head, again disgusted by her own tears, which always welled up when she most wanted composure. She lifted her glasses from her cheeks to wipe at her eyes.

"Lily," Mabel said softly, reaching across the table to touch at her elbow. Lily wished she didn't always bring out the sugary sweet pushiness in her sister. Lily had planned for it to be the other way around that night, for Mabel to be angry over Lily's decision to go find their ungrateful mother and for Lily to remain distant and consoling. *Mabel*, Lily would have said, gently taking her hand.

Lily thought of again reminding Mabel of that day their mother left them. Mabel had screamed and bawled, stumbling along the front walk of the antique shop, grasping at her mother's quick scissor-stepping legs. "Don't," their mother said, pushing at Mabel's head. Mabel grabbed the back strap of her mother's sandal, and she slapped Mabel's hand away. "Goddamn it, don't. I'm going to trip."

Lily had stayed on the front porch, not fully understanding. Her mother had not announced her departure, had only suddenly appeared in makeup and brushed hair, freshly ironed skirt and blouse, a small suitcase packed. As her mother rushed through the shop, her eyes to the ground, Lily sneezed from the breeze of heavy perfume. Mabel looked up from her comic book.

Mabel had known right away and had fallen suddenly into a fierce fit of crying. When their mother finally reached her car, she tossed her suitcase into the backseat, and Mabel reached in and tried to grab it back out. Their mother wrestled it from Mabel and tossed it back in. Mabel tried to get it back, but their mother held on to Mabel's sleeve in order to close the door.

"Give me a break, Mabel," her mother shouted at her. When the door slammed was when everything stopped. Mabel's screaming stopped; their mother's leaving stopped. They both stood still there next to the car, looking at each other with fear. Lily hadn't realized it just then, but the tip of Mabel's finger had caught in the door, and she'd pulled it out to hold her hand shaking before her. Her mouth was open wide, her jaw shivering, readying for the worst shriek of pain Lily would ever hear.

Though their mother lifted Mabel into her arms and seated the violently kicking girl in the front seat of the car, though she sped her to the emergency room for a few minutes of wrapping and splinting then brought her back to the shop to put her to bed and to lie beside her, nothing had changed her intentions. She slipped away for good after Mabel cried herself to sleep.

"You've been a mess yourself from time to time," Lily said, leaning back from the table. She took the lacy handkerchief that Mabel offered. Lily dried her cheeks, then held the hanky in her lap, running her finger along the cursive of the name of its original owner, "Penelope," embroidered at the edge.

"Lily," Mabel said, "why do you even want to see her? She doesn't care about us. She hasn't even called us in years. Did she even send me a birthday card? Does she even *remember* that it's my birthday?"

"So you mean to tell me," Lily said, "that you don't have the least bit of interest in seeing her again? Ever? There's nothing you want to know about her? Nothing you want to ask her?"

Mabel picked off a little corner of the birthday cake and ate it. "You're not going to learn anything. She's not going to tell you anything useful."

Lily tore off a bit of cake for herself. "You don't have to hate her so much. Our lives aren't ruined or anything. There's nothing wrong with us."

"There's nothing wrong, I know," Mabel repeated, almost beneath her breath.

"I think she meant to come back, don't you?" Lily didn't wait to let Mabel disagree. "I just think time may have passed differently for her. What seemed like forever to us, probably went very quickly for her. And, you know," Lily said, tearing off another edge of the cake, excited to be at her mother's defense, "it could be that she's been waiting for us to come find her."

"What the fuck were we supposed to do?" Mabel said,

raising her voice. "Crawl across the desert with our little plastic suitcases? With our grade-school watercolors . . . or our, you know, our fucking macaroni pictures for her to put on her fucking refrigerator? We were babies."

Lily was so relieved to hear Mabel's voice shake, to hear her sigh and cuss and to see her twisting her hair. Lily cocked her head with Mabel's gesture of concern and reached across the table to touch at her elbow.

"Shouldn't I at least go with you?" Mabel said, but she didn't wait for Lily to reject the offer. "Shouldn't we at least call her first?"

"We don't have her phone number."

"We could find it," Mabel said, "or we could send a telegram. But you don't want to do that, do you? You don't want to give her any warning."

Lily felt sorry for Mabel when she thought of her sitting alone in the house waiting for Jordan and Lily to come back. Mabel didn't really have any friends, and she'd never had a good boyfriend. "Just let me do this, Mabel," Lily nearly whispered. She took Mabel's hand to scratch affectionately at the chipped green polish of her fingernails. "I'm only going for a few days. I just want to introduce her to Jordan. Just take a walk with her. I just want to know her a little bit. I just want to get to know her."

Mabel pulled her hand away and stood from the table, brushing cake crumbs from the front of her dress. Silent, she walked toward the door of the bus. "Mabel," Lily said. "Mabel, don't be like that." Lily didn't go after her because she knew Mabel only ever needed a little bit of time. Mabel didn't like to cause worry for anything more than an hour or two. But when Lily saw that the Joan Armatrading album lay, still wrapped, beside the cake, she felt miserable for always disappointing poor Mabel. Lily tore off the tissue paper; she'd wrap it again later. She felt like hearing "Cool Blue Stole My Heart," so she unplugged the Christmas lights from the extension cord and plugged in the portable record player. In the near dark, she squinted at the turning record, looking for the right groove that started the song. As she set the needle down with a thump, Lily heard tiny stones tossed against the glass of the bus windows.

"Are you through being an asshole?" Jordan said, when Lily came to the window. Lily nodded, as pleased as always with Jordan's ease. She reached out the window for his cigarette, and he handed it up to her. She took a puff and handed it back. "Is Mabel mad?" he said.

"Yes," Lily said. "I want to go soon, Jordan." But she didn't trust that Starkweather's Packard would make it anywhere near Mexico.

Jordan reached up again and took Lily's hand. "We'll get the Packard tuned up," Jordan said, "then I'll take you to see your mother." Lily closed her eyes, liking the sound of that. Jordan, though skinny and wounded, could look after her very well if he set his mind to it. Feeling a buzz from the Manhattan and from the sugar of the cake, Lily was ready to believe in whatever Jordan told her.

"Come inside," Lily said.

Jordan returned to Lily's side at the table, and they ate some more cake with their fingers, ignoring the plastic forks and paper plates. "I ruined Mabel's birthday," Lily said.

"She'll be lonely when we're gone," Jordan said.

"Mabel will be fine," Lily said, and she really believed it. It would be best for the both of them to have some time apart. "We've always been fine. We've been lucky, really. We've always had a roof over our head." Jordan glanced up to the ceiling of the school bus with a skeptical half grin. "You know what I mean," Lily said.

Jordan leaned toward Lily to lick the frosting from the edge of her lips, then went back to sit on the bed to pull off his boots. Still at the table, her back to Jordan, Lily decided to finally ask him some questions she'd been avoiding. The questions, the most obvious ones, seemed like things she should have asked months before, on the third or fourth date or something. But it had been much easier not to, to let his steps toward suicide remain nothing more serious than a vague mystery.

"Did you hope to die that day?" Lily said, just said it, sitting in the dark not looking at him. "When you cut your wrist?" He didn't say anything for a moment, and Lily wondered if he was looking down at his scar, touching at it gently with his fingertip, tapping at it, uncertain it was his.

"Did I hope to die? Did I hope?" He said it snide, like it was the stupidest thing he'd ever heard. "No. No, I didn't hope to die. No. Fuck no." When Lily didn't say anything, Jordan continued, less peevish. "I was really young," he said, though the slashing of his wrist had only been a year or so before. "Everything seemed like a little more trouble than it was worth."

"You loved that girl," Lily said. "Kate." Lily wasn't bothered by Kate or by the creased picture of her he still kept tucked in a pocket of his wallet. In the photo, Kate sat in a bay window in an outdated white dress that had to have been hand-me-down. The black braid of her hair lay across her shoulder, and her silver heart-shaped locket was open at her throat. Lily had never met Kate, but she respected her as part of Jordan's heartbreak, part of why he was the way he was.

"When she said it was over," Jordan said, "I thought about dying and thought about how if I died, I'd at least be something important in her life. It would change her forever, wouldn't it? It got so I liked thinking of myself as a pretty girl's dead boyfriend. I figured I'd be some ghost, and I'd watch her grow old and sad. I'd see her never quite getting over it all." Jordan sighed, then began tapping his fingers to the song on the record. "But hell, yeah, I'm glad I didn't die. She was kind of a toothy girl, really, and, you know, she didn't really dance as well as she thought she did."

Lily imagined telling her mother exactly what Jordan had said about not wanting to die, as they had one of those long breakfasts that last past lunch, as they talked about their days apart.

She went to sit beside Jordan on the bed. She pictured him wet and sleepy in the tub, his arm flung out in tragic gesture, his cheeks tear-streaked. A beautiful waste, Lily thought, feeling dramatic imagining his blood *drip drip dripping* into a puddle on the peeling linoleum floor. A wasteful beauty.

Lily took Jordan's hand and touched at the scar, and she knew that it was a bright pink declaration of life, no matter what he said about death and becoming a ghost—he'd cut only one wrist just minutes before his mother was expected home from work. Not only did Jordan not want to die, Lily realized, but he wanted to be begged to live.

9.

MABEL AND LILY'S MOTHER HAD LEFT in the spring, a few days after Easter. They had gone to church that Easter morning. Their mother had turned religious in the few months after their father's death and had pilfered the shop for all its sacred relics: the plastic dashboard virgins, the votive candles, the strings of rosary beads, the pictures of angels, the lives of the saints. Mabel's grandmother had robbed many abandoned country churches over the years, prying shiny crosses from pulpits with the flat of a screwdriver or stealing panes of stained glass to put up for sale. Mabel had been with her at some of these churches and had wandered the graveyards, fearful her grandmother would come out with a shovel and start turning up dirt to get at a ribbon in wiry hair and to pluck a brooch from a rotting chest.

On the way back from Easter service, just as they passed

the ANTIQUES 1 MI. sign, a sandhill crane lifted its gangly body from the weeds of the ditch and unfolded into something enormous. For a moment, Mabel heard nothing, not the engine of the car, not the wheels, nothing but the flap of the heavy wings, like the sound of a sheet in the wind on the laundry line. Mabel's mother tried to swerve away from the crane, but swerved into it, and its talons scratched the glass of the windshield. Mabel heard it hit the roof and roll across, and when her mother slammed on the brakes, Lily fell forward. Everyone was fine, though Lily had a few scratches from the sharp-edged dash. When they stepped from the car, they found only feathers and blood, but no bird on the ground or in the sky.

Mabel, imagining the crane broken and near death somewhere in the dried yellow weeds of the ditch, began to search for it. She picked up a stalk of milkweed and poked at the ditch, hoping to rustle the bird out. Before Mabel could find any sign of anything, Lily burst into tears. A drop of blood had fallen from the scratch of her brow into her eye, and her mother scooped her up into her arms and put her back in the car.

"We'll come back to look for the bird," her mother told Mabel, but Mabel knew they wouldn't. Once they were back to the house, her mother would collapse into bed and would sleep until Tuesday. Mabel took one last jab at the ditch, then set the milkweed stalk at the edge of the road where she could easily pick it up again when she returned to her search. As they drove away, Mabel looked out the back window, wondering what could be done for an injured bird. Mabel would need bandages, she thought, and a bowl for the crane to drink from. She would prepare a nest of blankets and down pillows in the back of the old Buick up on blocks in the pasture.

When they got the inconsolable Lily up to the bedroom, Mabel's concerns switched to her sister. Mabel's mother undressed Lily and dabbed the scratches on her cheeks and hands with a pale silver ointment. Lily's gentle sobs dropped her into sleep. When their mother left the room, Mabel stripped naked in sympathy and ran her finger along the scratches on Lily's skin, picking up some of the ointment on her fingertip. She dabbed the ointment onto a days-old scratch of her own.

Mabel smelled Lily's sleeping breath—peppermint from the leaves she liked to chew. She whispered in Lily's ear. "Tara's dead," she whispered, "Jenny's dead . . . Sally's dead . . . Brenda's dead," a soft litany of Lily's friends and cousins, all still living and healthy. Mabel hoped to stir up nightmares in Lily's sleep. Sometimes, in the middle of the night, Lily would wake crying, and Mabel would hold her sister in her arms and stroke her hair.

Mabel blew Lily's fine hair from her face, and she kissed her cheek, then her shoulder, then her naked hip.

Lily whimpered in her sleep, and twitched. Mabel ran her fingers along Lily's stomach, touched at her knob-like belly button. Lily wore a rusty spoon twisted around her wrist like a bracelet, and Mabel ran her finger along its bend.

Bored with her own nakedness, Mabel went to the closet

for a robe. The light from the shop downstairs seeped up between the floorboards, and she touched her toe to the light as she crossed the room. She put on a tattered robe her mother had passed down to her, though it was much too big. She pressed her ear to the wall and she listened for the religious songs turned languid in her mother's deep singing voice that broke and gave the songs an unintended intimacy—as if Jesus were someone her mother had known, someone she'd touched. But the house was silent.

Sitting on the floor, Mabel ate supermarket blackberries one-by-one from a bowl on the nightstand. The berries were hard and sour, but Mabel decided she liked them that way. It seemed grown-up to like the taste of things that tasted bad. She remembered sitting on her father's lap, a cigarette dangling from his lips, and she'd closed her mouth around the awful smoke. She'd stolen sips from her father's beer and thought it tasted of moldy bread.

Mabel was not Mabel's real name; she'd chosen it after her father killed himself. Many nights her father had come home and had winked and said to her mother, "What's cooking, Mabel," though her mother's name wasn't Mabel, and she never cooked at night. He'd call her Mabel at other times, like when he thought the girls were in bed and no one else could see him or hear him, standing in a towel in the hallway after an evening bath. He'd call her mother Mabel and he'd put his hand in her blouse and he'd kiss her neck and whisper in her hair, his breath the smell of the anise seeds and baking powder he used to brush his teeth, the way he'd brushed his teeth in his Catholic boy's school. Though Lily and their mother never complained about calling Mabel by her new name, they did at times seem startled by the sound of it, would jump as if they heard Mabel's father's deep morning cough again on the other side of the bedroom wall.

Mabel's father had been an insomniac, and Mabel had sat up with him many nights as he fretted and drank Alka-Seltzer for his nervous stomach. Sometimes they'd play rummy; sometimes he'd just talk to her, telling her about what he thought his life would be like someday. He thought he might like to take some courses and become a stage technician. He had played Mitch in *A Streetcar Named Desire* in high school, and people had told him how much they'd liked him in the part. But it was ridiculous to think of becoming an actor, he knew. So he'd hang lights for local presentations and plays, paint sets, and even sew costumes. Sometimes his eyes were red and wet, and he rubbed at them and sniffled, and Mabel never knew if he was crying or just sleepy. If Mabel would start to drift off, her father would make a pot of coffee and give her a cup with lots of milk and tablespoons of sugar. He'd go on about some other things, like how his parents always loved his brother more and how he'd done some drugs in school and how he'd wanted Mabel's mother to have an abortion, but was now so glad that she hadn't, because he loved Mabel so much and couldn't imagine how things would be without her. But he did imagine things without her, again and again, as he described a life he'd have if he didn't have responsibilities.

Mabel picked up Lily's glasses from the nightstand and put them on, and everything in the room stepped forward and large into her sight. The black wardrobe, its doors gaping open, threatened the room like a cornered beast. The glasses gave Mabel a headache and she took them off and the room fell back again, everything, again, what it was supposed to be. Mabel wondered if Lily needed these glasses in order to notice the world at all. Mabel thought of her grandmother's friend, a blind woman in black-lensed, octagonal spectacles. "I'm very blind," the woman said just the day before, "but I know there have been changes in the atmosphere. In the mornings, I sense a difference in the light of my room." Maybe that was all the impression life made on Lily, Mabel thought, an impression as slight as the shifting of shadow and color.

Mabel's mother carried in a tray with two plates of pancakes. Lily loved pancakes, even for her dinner and supper. Her mother set the tray on a trunk and hesitantly touched Lily's shoulder. "Lily?" she whispered, then cringed. "Lily?" Sometimes Lily slapped or kicked the person waking her. "Lily?" she whispered, even more softly. Her mother looked to Mabel. "Should I leave her sleep?" she said, and Mabel said, "Yes."

"What?" her mother said, as if she hadn't expected a voice, as if she'd only been asking the room or a ghost in the room. She then left the plates on an old piano bench long since separated from its piano, and she skulked away. Mabel was very hungry and ate both pancakes before Lily woke.

Lily sat up in bed. "What flew up out of the ditch?" she said, in a choked, waking voice.

"It was a crane," Mabel told Lily.

"It was something worse than a crane," Lily said, pulling at a sheet and covering her naked body up to her chin. Mabel thought Lily might be right; all the cranes had passed through weeks before, before it had even turned spring. Hundreds had died with ice in their feathers. Mabel had seen it on the news—a man lifting a frozen crane from a frozen tree, then tossing the carcass atop other carcasses in the back of a pickup truck. It broke Mabel's heart even more to think of her crane in the ditch, having survived the ice only to get hit on her family's Sunday morning drive.

"I'm hungry," Lily said, standing from the bed with her sheet still wrapped around her. She hid behind the closet door to change into a sundress with a daisy print. Lily had newly found this modesty, and Mabel was convinced she was only pretending. She just wanted to hurt Mabel, to hide her round, plump body away and leave Mabel alone with her terrible bones and sickly olive skin. The old farmers' wives and widows frequently descended upon the house to weigh and measure Mabel. Though they never marked down any measurement, they were certain, with each visit, some fraction of a fraction of an inch had dissolved from her body. They examined her in her underwear. One old woman, who wore long skirts and always held a white stone pipe, constantly unlit, in her long fingers, would tap that pipe at the knobs of Mabel's shoulders and elbows, sending a ringing down through all her bones. But Lily they pinched and adored, admiring of the way she moved indifferently about them all like a rowdy cherub.

In the few months since their father had died, Lily had wanted to be close to Mabel. They had spoken that winter in a mock sign language, wiggling their fingers in the air and pretending to understand each other. They'd faked silent conversation at breakfast and at dinner, even outside in the cold, their fingers hidden by mittens. But now, with the spring thaw, Lily had changed. *I'll only love you more*, she seemed to be saying, *if you don't look at me, if you don't speak to me, if you don't touch me, if you don't know me*.

Mabel followed Lily into the hall, and down to their mother's room. The door was closed and locked. Lily pressed her lips to the keyhole. "We're hungry," she said. Their mother spent much of her time sleeping in her bed. The only reason they'd gone out that Easter morning was because Pastor Lenny had been by a few days before. He'd told their mother that Mabel and Lily desperately needed the guidance of church. He'd spoken so loudly, his voice coming up from so deep in his throat and his chest, it had seemed he'd blow the whole house down with his prayer. If she and Lily were minister's daughters, Mabel thought, they could steal a wafer and lick it. They could explore all the mysteries of the altar—take a sip from the baptismal font, blow out the everlasting flame and inhale its curl of smoke.

"Come downstairs," Mabel said. She felt guilty for eating Lily's pancake. "I'll find you something."

Downstairs, Lily sat at a table in a corner of the shop, and

Mabel went to the kitchen. The kitchen was nothing but a narrow closet lit by one faint bulb. Mabel looked into the refrigerator and found only uncooked ham wrapped in newspaper and a jar of apple rings. "She has to eat something," Mabel said aloud, plucking the mold from a slice of bread, then opening a can of sardines found in a drawer.

The table was still set for tea from the day before. In the teapot, tea bags steeped in black water and a horsefly did a dead-man's float in someone's half-empty cup. The day before, as usual, Lily had ignored the old women who gathered with their grandmother for bridge and stood on a chair with a key to wind all the clocks on the wall. It was as if Lily knew her clock-winding would drop the women into quiet and hesitance, would turn them reflective, pondering what a young girl winding clocks might mean to their old lives. Above the thick ticking grown noisome in the room, Mrs. Beard said, "Mr. Beard thinks he's finished his breakfast before I've even cooked it. He's dressed for bed hours before he's tired. He doesn't even know a clock anymore." As she spoke of how she was teaching him time again, her spotted and wrinkled fingers gracefully drew a clock in the air, creating a round face and the long and short hands, casting fragile shadows against the wall. But Mabel was anxious for old age; she admired the old women's resignation and knowledge. She thought it must be a powerful thing to know for certain that you wouldn't die young.

When Mabel brought Lily her sandwich on a plate, Lily said, "Take it away." She performed a lethargic puppet show for herself with two raggedy puppets that normally hung from nails in the wall. "Fish," Lily said in the shrill, disgusted voice of the puppet on her left hand, a sailor in a cap. The sailor lay a lazy kiss against the head of the other puppet, a Spanish señorita. Then Lily lowered her hands and let the puppets slip off to the floor.

"I thought you said you were hungry," Mabel said. "You have to eat."

Lily held her fat fingers in the air, pinching at the imagined lid of a pot, holding its handle, then pantomimed the pouring of tea. She smiled sweetly and mouthed polite conversation to the absent guests. She then expertly peeled a fictional orange.

Annoyed by being left out of Lily's silent party, Mabel began to noisily clear the table, stacking cups and saucers onto a tray. Bent at the back, she carried the tray to the kitchen. She happened to look out the window and saw people in the old Riordan house on the hill. One wall of the abandoned house had fallen away with the weight of the last heavy snow, and all its insides were exposed. There was nothing to see but the bare wood of walls and floors, the squares where doors and windows had been. But only a few days before, as Mabel had walked up the hill, examining in the palm of her hand the husk of a locust, she happened to glance up just as the sun shifted. The house filled, for only a second, with a sharp light, and shadows of things not there fell and moved.

Mabel took the opera glasses from the windowsill and looked at the people in the Riordan house. They tiptoed over the floor like walking across an icy pond. They bent, picked things up, put things in their pockets. Mabel hated that they found things to take; she'd been through the house several times and had found only the chipped enamel of a piano key. One woman even climbed the stairs to the second floor, something Mabel had been much too afraid to do. The woman appeared weightless and undisturbed walking across the weak wood planks of the floor that was barely there.

Suddenly, Mabel worried that these women were bird-watchers, part of one of the many groups that passed through looking for cranes and herons and prairie chickens. She put the opera glasses in the pocket of her robe and headed for the front door, determined to go find her wounded crane before these women did. She wanted to be the one to care for it, to nurse it back into flight.

A fire engine, as it wailed past, shook the road next to the shop, and the rows of empty perfume bottles and atomizers jingled against each other. At the kitchen window, Mabel saw the smoke rising from a neighboring field. In the last week, farmers had been burning the old stalks from their fields before plowing, and sometimes the wind, with a mean-spirited twist, would shift directions and send the flame somewhere unintended. Mabel already missed winter, missed breaking the brittle stumps of cornstalks beneath her heavy winter boots. In winter, when the wind blew and the snow on the plains broke like dust, she couldn't tell where the ground ended and the sky began. But on quiet, windless days, Mabel could nearly hear the smoke leaving the chimney.

As Mabel looked for her coat at the front of the shop, Lily stood, grinning, in front of the wall of clocks. "What?" Mabel said. Lily looked Mabel directly in the eyes for the first time in weeks. She held something in her mouth. "What do you have?" Mabel said. Lily kept silent, then slowly pointed to the Swiss clock that hadn't worked for years. On the tiny wheel beneath the face, the tiny woodsman still stood, his ax still lifted, but the little girl with braids was gone.

Mabel had always wanted to steal the little girl from the clock, to hide it in a chamois bag. Lily tugged on the sleeve of Mabel's robe, the little wooden girl on her stuck-out tongue. Mabel wanted to rip the tongue clean from Lily's head.

"Why did you take that?" Mabel said, but she already knew the answer. Lily broke the clock because Mabel wouldn't. How had Lily even known Mabel wanted the little girl? It seemed it should have been nothing but inconsequential to everyone else. But Lily, with her hateful instinct, knew. Lily took her tongue, and the girl, back into her mouth.

Mabel made a fist, lifted it to her shoulder, and punched Lily. She only barely hit Lily's ear, but it startled Lily, and she fell, hitting her head against the table before dropping to the floor. Lily's glasses were knocked from her face, and Mabel noticed a new scratch beneath her eye that slowly reddened with blood. But Lily didn't cry; she sat with her mouth open, nodding her head quickly like a clucking chicken. When she brought her hands up to press at her own throat, Mabel realized she was choking on the wooden girl. Mabel was too frightened to scream, though she wanted to, and she spun around in a circle, looking all along the walls of the shop for some suggestion of what to do. Lily opened her mouth wide to Mabel, as if expecting her to reach in.

Mabel found her voice and shouted up the stairs for her mother, uncertain that she would even respond. But her mother did come running from her room, her door slamming into the wall as she threw it open. She hurried down the stairs and, needing no explanation, she put her hands beneath Lily's arms and lifted her to her feet, then put her hands above Lily's stomach and squeezed her as if she was a bagpipe. The little wooden girl popped from Lily's mouth and flew away to be lost in the clutter of the shop.

"That's it," their mother said matter-of-factly as Lily coughed. She licked her thumb and wiped the blood from Lily's cheek.

"Is she all right?" Mabel said, but she was already so relieved. She was relieved that Lily no longer choked and that it was her mother who saved her. Her mother's cheeks had color, and she stood up straight and ran her fingers through Lily's hair, scowling at the terrible rat's nest it had become.

"When was the last time you had a bath?" she said, kneeling to take Lily into her arms, pressing her lips against her forehead. "You're all right," she told her, sounding convincing for the first time in weeks. "You're lucky. People choke on things all the time. I should know, I used to be a waitress."

"She choked on the little Swiss girl from the clock," Mabel said, gently pinching Lily's shoulder as apology for hitting her. "I wonder where it went?"

"We need to find it," their mother said, jumping up and setting Lily on her feet. "We need to put it back on the clock before your grandmother gets back. You girls have to stop running roughshod over this place."

Punish us, Mabel thought. *Spank us. Correct us*. As the three of them moved about the shop, they picked things up and put things back and quickly became distracted from their mission. Lily tried on an old felt hat and pulled the lace of it down over her face. Mabel's mother sorted through a box of reading spectacles, testing different pairs by holding them before her eyes and reading from a framed list of hotel laws. Mabel opened the drawer of an apothecary and took from it a cornshuck doll, its skirt half eaten by mites. Mabel then sat on the floor next to a chest full of single, unmatched shoes, and she tried each one on. Lily pressed the dents from the plastic head of a doll.

They lifted things, examined them, then put them in the wrong places; they scooted aside tables and chairs to make paths for themselves; they picked up boxes to look in the boxes beneath them. The shop, a secondhand shop where nothing ever changed hands, where the prices had all faded from the tags, possessed an order and permanence Mabel relied upon. It was as if the layers of dust and webs that covered everything anchored everything to the floor. Mabel had even hidden things of her own in the shop—there was a letter, from her Aunt Phyll, folded up and tucked behind a hat band; inside a toaster was a honeymoon photo of her mother and father in front of Mount Rushmore. Mabel even kept the pieces of a busted record, a recording, made in a booth at the state fair, of her father singing an old song—"Chuck E.'s in Love." Mabel had hidden the pieces inside a long, white glove inside a long, yellow box.

Lily's act of theft, Mabel thought, her taking the little wooden girl, had changed something in the house, had changed the gravity in the room, lifting their mother from her bed. Mabel looked to the ceiling, worried about the chairs and rolls of carpet tied to the rafters with frayed rope and knots that hadn't been tightened in years.

They all quickly bored of their search and collapsed into a dusty sofa. Mabel rested her head in her mother's lap; Lily lay against her shoulder. Mabel felt so at ease. For weeks, she had been too worried about them all to feel at all safe. She feared that, with her mother shut up in her room, her grandmother off robbing old farms and churches, that someone would sneak in to steal Lily away, to molest her; they wouldn't take Mabel because she was too thin and prickly, but Lily they would find adorable. Someday, Lily would be found in the city, feral and dirty and mute. Mabel would be brought in to coax her from her silence. She would dress up in a gray wool skirt and a white blouse with a bit of lace at the tips of the collar. She'd ask private questions only a sister could ask. She'd ask Lily in a quiet voice, "Where did they touch you?" She'd ask, "What did they make you touch?"

Lily took the plastic cork from a small vial and sprinkled some perfume on her wrist. She ran her wrist along her neck and chest. She then held the vial before her eyes to try to read the faint lettering, but even with her glasses so thick, she seemed unable to make it out. "Wild Skin," Lily pretended to read, though Mabel could see that it said only "Do not drink."

Mabel, so exhausted she drifted into a minute's sleep, saw her father's eyes as pale green as Coke bottle glass, and his open mouth, and she heard the gun knock against his teeth. She woke with a gasp, and her mother said, "Shhhh," and smoothed back Mabel's hair. Mabel wondered if her father killed himself because her mother refused to ever see him again. He probably loved her so much.

Lily held her hand to her throat and sighed, affecting their mother's posture of grief. "My nerves are shot," she muttered.

They heard the rumble of an old car pass on the road alongside the shop, and they all rushed to the window to look out. An apricot-colored Toronado glistened like jam in a pot. Crammed into the car were the women, the birdwatchers Mabel had seen walking through the Riordan house. A ways down the first mile, the car slowed. Mabel took the opera glasses from her pocket and she could see the women spill from the car to investigate; Mabel held one hand over her heart beating hard as the women picked up the bloody feathers from the ground. Her mother held tightly to Mabel's hand, and Lily pressed her hand against the glass of the window.

Each birdwatcher headed off in a different direction, slowly searching a different parcel of land. Worse than them finding the bird dead, Mabel thought, would be them finding it alive. Then they'd all know that someone had left it there alone to suffer unrepaired.

5.

ON THE NIGHT OF HER BIRTHDAY, after leaving Lily's school-bus apartment, Mabel got in the Jimmy and drove away. She recognized every field and fence post her headlights swept across. Some people thought of it all as open spaces of nothing, and that's what made the land feel close to Mabel's heart. She knew the rhythms of the rattling planks as she drove across old wood bridges, and she knew which roads were heavily rutted from heavy farm machinery. She knew which corners hid dangerous blind spots and which railroad tracks had no red lights of warning. She knew intimately a nearly private part of the world. There was a kind of privilege in that, Mabel decided.

Mabel drove to the Platte River, to where her father liked to take them all for a swim beneath the bridge. After they'd given up on chasing the bull the night of her eighth birthday, after the bull had run across the graveyard and into the dark behind the white church, escaping entirely, they'd gone to the river. Mabel's father parked at the edge of the bridge and they all stumbled out of the pickup. He flipped forward the seat and took a flashlight from a toolbox and two warm beers from a paper sack. He gave a beer to Mabel's mother, who held Lily asleep in her arms, then took Mabel by the hand.

"Did I ever show you this?" he said, shining the light before them, leading her to a thick wooden post partly broken and slightly bent. He pressed her fingers to the break, to a spot of blue paint. "When your mom went into labor with you, I was out here getting drunk with the guys. Your grandpa came out to tell me, and I was so out of it and so excited that I got in my car and thought I was going in reverse, but I was going forward. I ran into this post and knocked my head against the steering wheel or something. Knocked myself out and cut myself up and made a wreck of my car. Ten stitches," he said, shining the flashlight on the little scar on his forehead. He'd told her about it all before, but she liked hearing it again and touching his scar. She liked hearing about how her birth, a month too soon, disrupted everything. "When I came to, I just walked down the hall to the nursery to look in at you. You were all squinty and fuzzy and crabby in your crib. A fussy little mess. But who can blame you, you'd just been through a lot."

Mabel drove the Jimmy up to the post, still bent and broken. She got out and knelt beside the break and touched at the bit of blue paint that remained. Above the rush of the water over the sand, Mabel heard wind whistling through the holes in the bridge, and she thought of the blades of grass her father would pluck from the side of the river. He'd put the grass between his teeth for sharp, quick whistles that neither Mabel nor Lily could reproduce when he placed the grass on their tongues.

Mabel stood and leaned against the post and worried about her father on that day of her birth. He was drunk and clumsy and could have been hurt worse, leaving Mabel even sooner than he had, leaving her without Lily, even. But what business did he have having babies and leaving his friends on a warm summer day at the river? He was only a kid, still knocking himself around, getting stitches in his head. Mabel took off her shoes and stepped into the river water, and the feel of sand between her toes and the bite of a minnow at her ankle reminded her of how her father had dangled her over the side of the bridge when she was very small. He'd hold tight to her feet and dip her toward the river and she'd stretch to touch the water's top. Feeling the wind, and the spin of the blood rushing to her head as the river flowed beneath her, Mabel felt that her only connection to earth was the little bit of pain from her father's grip too tight. By the time she turned eight, she'd gotten too big, too heavy for her father's bad shoulders ruined in high school football. She sometimes begged her father, and her mother would scold her for begging, and she'd end up wasting the afternoon pouting, wishing she was only five or six again.

AS MABEL drove back home, she opened the glove compartment to look for a box of Hot Tamales left from the last time she went to the movies, and she saw a newspaper clipping she'd saved for Lily. One of the old farm women, who knew Mabel's habit of collecting tragic stories, had given the clipping to her a few weeks before.

Mabel read the article as she drove, holding it up to the dashboard light. A ten-year-old girl was taken to a therapist for something called rebirth therapy that involved wrapping the girl in blankets and pillows. The therapist twisted the girl up in the blanket to represent the womb and pressed on the pillows to simulate labor contractions. The girl suffocated and died. *Troubled*, the article said about the girl. "*The therapy is intended to enable troubled children to heal from past trauma.*" Mabel was sick thinking about what miseries the poor little girl had endured, probably again and again, at the hands of irresponsible adults.

Mabel drove the pickup right up to the side of the bus, leaving the headlights on. She stepped up into the bus and up to the mattress, where Lily, covering herself with a sheet, squinted and held her hand up to the light.

"Lily," Mabel said, pushing aside the mosquito netting and kneeling beside the bed. Jordan grumbled in his sleep and rolled over.

"Sweetie," Lily said, wiping some tears from Mabel's cheeks with the palm of her hand. "Sweetheart."

"I have an idea. I just thought of it as I drove up, just now." Mabel paused for effect, taking hold of Lily's arm. She'd never been more serious about anything. "A foster child. We could take in a foster child. You know, some fucked-up little mess who nobody has ever loved. I mean, I just thought of it just now, but it's so friggin' perfect." Mabel, distracted by her new idea, didn't care what Lily did or where she went. Mabel wanted to go up to the house immediately and scrounge through the shop for children's toys, for little dresses or pants. She wanted to get a room ready for her new, miserably sad son or daughter.

"Jordan," Lily said, shaking at him. "Go turn off those headlights." Jordan crawled out of bed in his boxer shorts and sleepily kissed Mabel on the top of the head as he passed her. "Lie down here," Lily said.

"I can't, Lily," Mabel said. "There are things I want to do up at the house."

"They're not going to let you have a kid," Lily said. "You have to meet income requirements and stuff. You have to have stability. You're too young. I mean, someday you'll make a great foster parent, but now you just need to lie down. Come on, I'm tired." The bus fell into darkness as Jordan put out the headlights. Mabel heard Lily making room for her on the mattress.

"No," Mabel said, "no, Lily, see, that's where you're wrong. There are more of these fucked-up kids than they know what to do with. And, see, I'll take anybody in. It doesn't have to be some cute little kid, I'll take some bitchy fourteen-year-old drug addict. I've got a lot to offer somebody like that." Mabel felt winded from her argument, but she kept with it, her voice weakening, her breathing hard. "I'm not too young. I had to grow up really fast." But she knew she didn't sound convincing.

Jordan got back into bed on the other side of Lily, and Lily took Mabel's arm, pulling her in. Mabel, too tired to object, and still in her shoes and her dress, lay beside Lily. She lay on her back, feeling Lily's breath on her neck. "I went to the river," Mabel said. "I heard Dad whistling. I really did."

"I'm too tired to play," Lily said. "Go to sleep." Though it was much too hot to be lying so close, Mabel drifted off at Lily's command, the newspaper clipping still crumpled in her fist.

6.

AT CARUSO'S STEAK-AND-SPAGHETTI house on the square in Bonnevilla, Jordan strummed a guitar as part of a guitar trio that trolled about the tables for tips and song requests. Lily waitressed and ran the cigar counter, selling the Palmas and the Pencils and the Churchill Sweets.

A long bench sat along one wall of the lobby of the steakhouse, and the same handful of men gathered there nightly. They spent hours tossing cards into an overturned hat in some lazy game. As they talked, smoke lifted from their lips with every word or laugh or wheeze, and the minutes they burned from the ends of their lives clouded the lobby.

Lily closed up the cigar counter and slapped her hands toward the old men on the bench, like shooing pigeons. When she turned her back on them, she felt somebody's bony fingers brush across her ass, and a shudder of death worked through her. It outraged her that even one of them thought they could touch her with their rotten-corpse hands, and "Which one of you ratty fucking dogs . . ." was what she wanted to say, but her boss still sat at his corner desk counting his day's dollars, smoking a long, fat Excalibur.

Lily locked up the glass humidors on the counter and heard the clink and churn of the toy vending machine by the front door. "Anything good?" Lily asked Jordan. He examined the small plastic globe that fell from the chute and took from it a sheet of lick-on tattoos. He placed a picture of a hula girl on his tongue then lifted the sleeve of Lily's dress and pressed the wet paper against the skin of her upper arm.

Lily held her sleeve up and blew on the tattoo to dry it; she winked at Jordan, charmed by his gift of the hula girl. She gave Jordan a lot of grief a lot of the time, but he was irresistible, mostly, like his attraction to old comics bought from used bookstores. Though he read the Daredevil, and Ghost Rider, and Silver Surfer, it was his taste for Hot Stuff, and Baby Huey, and Little Lotta that attracted Lily. She had thought it adorable one day when she'd gone in for a pedicure and found Jordan sitting at his manicurist's table sipping from a cup of Thera-Flu tea and reading Spooky, the Tuff Little Ghost.

"A guy who was just in here said there's an abandoned house burning to the ground in the country," Jordan said. "Everybody's driving out to watch it."

Lily followed Jordan out the alley door. Jordan looked handsome and reckless to Lily, his guitar strapped to his back, a few crazy notes plinking from the strings with his walking. The double breast of Jordan's blue uniform was unbuttoned, and he held a bottle of something to his thin, naked chest. The uniform was from an old high school band, complete with braided epaulets; the restaurant owner had bought it at the hospital thrift.

When they got in the Packard, Jordan held out the bottle, a raspberry-flavored schnapps. "Want a sip?"

"Ick," Lily said. "You're a mess with all your sweet stuff. Rot your teeth and your gut." When Lily first met Jordan, she thought him a cute ruin.

"You've got some wrong ideas about me," Jordan said.

A portable tape deck sat on the floor of the Packard, and Lily turned it on. When she heard Chrissie Hynde singing, she took the tape from the deck and saw her father's handwriting across the white label of the cassette. The tape was one of many Lily's father had left behind. Lily thought it was sweet that Jordan would have this with him, would play something like "Brass in Pocket" even when alone.

Lily's father had some musical talent, she remembered; he could play a song on the piano, just having heard it once. Often, when Lily heard a new song, she could hear an echo, a spirit accompaniment—a tinny rendering on an untuned piano. For six months, Lily's father rented an upright painted over a hideous brownish green. When the music store called one rainy Saturday afternoon to say someone was coming by to repossess it, Lily's father tossed together a block party in the apartment living room. Lily hadn't been very old at the time, but she remembered it all, and the details of the party continued to break her heart. She remembered the neighbors' umbrellas and galoshes in the hallway, and how, when she touched the apartment walls, she could feel them shivering with the laughs and chatter of all the guests crammed in the tiny room. Her father broke out bottles of Champale (*A drink so fine*, Eddy Rollow proclaimed with his trademark wink, *it's given to departing contestants on game shows*) and he took requests. Even Lily's mother, who'd been too depressed those days to leave the loveseat, asked Eddy to play a song from *Yentl*. She put on a gauzy yellow tea-length and a cloth rose in her hair, and she drank her Champale with tomato juice.

Had Lily's mother attempted suicide herself one late night? Lily wasn't sure, but she thought she remembered lying in bed, hearing her mother coughing and retching and her father's urgent tones muffled by the phone receiver. Had it been that same night that Mrs. Black from across the hall had come in to give Lily and Mabel baby aspirin and to read to them from *Ramona the Pest* until they fell asleep? Lily took a pen from her purse and wrote MOM—SUICIDE? on the palm of her hand. She was keeping a list of terribly sensitive questions she'd ask when she finally saw her mother again.

Lily took a pack of cigarettes from her purse and offered Jordan a Virginia Slim. Jordan shook his head and bit the tip off another Pixy Stix. He poured the powder into his mouth. "No dirty cheroot shall ever perch atop this lip again," Jordan said.

"I don't know what you're saying half the time," Lily said,

but she put her cigarettes away. It was too hot to smoke. Everyone was quitting.

"I'll still love you when you've got a hole in your throat," Jordan said. "And when your lungs are black, you'll still be just as pretty to me." He'd quit smoking only a few days before and already become quite pious about it.

Jordan drove west of town, toward the tufts of smoke blacker than the night sky and rising high above the tall corn in the fields. A long row of cars was parked facing the burning house, and some boys got drunk in a ditch. Lily and Jordan parked and sat on the hood of the Packard. The car's new black paint reflected the movement of the fire. Jordan plucked an ash from Lily's cheek.

Once upon a time, a woman named Mrs. Bixby lived in this house, and she invited Lily and Mabel to pick the wild plums from the trees in the back. The girls tied dishtowels around their heads and wore aprons, and they stepped over what seemed a whole city of lazy dogs lying in the dirt. Mrs. Bixby's house had been very old even then, its white walls already marked black by a past fire. The plums had too many seeds for the tastes of Lily and Mabel, so they left their apronfuls of pickings with Mrs. Bixby, who cooked the plums and preserved them, then presented the jars of jam to the girls late in the summer. Lily remembered walking home with the jars still cold from Mrs. Bixby's fridge, and she had rolled the glass along her hot neck and chest.

The heat of the burning house made Lily's neck tingle, and she reached back to push her hair up. Her glasses slid down in the sweat of her nose. Lily saw a little deeper into Mrs. Bixby's past then: a buffalo-head nickel in a penny loafer; a ring weighing down the front pocket of a man's shirt. Lily had a hint of psychic ability and she'd been trying to hone it, reading books on the reading of tarot and tea leaves. She kept a small book on palmistry in her purse and had been skimming it during the slow hours at work.

When Lily turned away from the burning house, all she saw was the pitch black of unlit roads and fields. She often felt claustrophobic in the country, pressed-in by the emptiness. On moonless, starless nights, when you couldn't see far, it seemed you could reach out and press your hand flat against the dark.

When Lily was little, she'd always worried about how she would direct fire trucks to her grandmother's house in the country. Their only address was Rural Route One, and Lily had always anticipated a fire from the furnace beneath the floor of the shop. Lily and Mabel had felt drawn to drop things through the grating in the middle of the front room. They pretended someone kept a girl prisoner in the bowels of the house, and they squatted down at the grating and dropped in sticks of gum and notes that said things like "someone will save you soon." Lily's other grandparents, her father's parents, lived at 4214 California Street in Omaha. If 4214 California were to start on fire, neighbors would arrive with buckets and hoses. The firemen would find their way easily; 4-2-1-4 in silver hung above the porch.

Jordan played a tune on his guitar, a tune Lily recognized

after a minute. It was from a record, a Phoebe Snow, Lily's father used to play.

Jordan stopped singing suddenly and put the guitar aside. "The strings are too hot," he said. He called for one of the boys in the ditch to toss up some ice. The boy flung across the hood of the car a handful of cubes from his Styrofoam cooler. Lily picked up a cube and tossed it from hand to hand. Jordan leaned over to kiss Lily on the cheek. She jumped, shocked from the cold of his lips. She kissed his lips, running her tongue along the ice in his mouth.

Lily leaned back against the front window of the car, taking a few milagros from her pocket: the tiny flat body, head to foot, of a girl in a skirt; a round stomach with a belly button at its center. She put the stomach milagro in her mouth and tasted it for words unspoken in her mother's letter. This last letter with the details of the nuns' kindnesses and the beautiful vineyard seemed as phony to Lily as her father's suicide note. Her mother had always before written of the squalor of her life, of mean lovers and no money and American tourists shot down in front of saloons and bookie joints. What had changed Lily's mother? Why, all of a sudden, was she so willing to admit to some happiness? Lily would have to remember to write that question down.

Lily had changed her mind about wanting a quiet reunion. Mabel was right—their mother probably wanted nothing to do with them. There would have to be fight and drama, at least some. It would be dishonest to be polite. When Lily arrived at the vineyard, she would not avoid the intimate and the painful. Lily and her mother could spend days thrashing it out good until they arrived at satisfying conclusions.

"If you were to steal Mrs. Bixby's car," Lily told Jordan, "I might let you take me away tonight." The old barn, far back from the burning house, still stood. A few years before, Mrs. Bixby had named Lily a good price for the good-condition 1985 Monte Carlo she never drove anymore.

"I'm not a thief," Jordan said, picking up his guitar. He played it, using a sliver of ice as a pick. "No . . . wait a minute." He made like he was sucking on something, working his jaw around, then pulled from his lips a silver bracelet. The trick made Lily think of the fairy tale about the two sisters; when the good sister spoke, rosebuds and diamonds and strings of pearls fell from her lips, but the bad sister spoke in toads and snakes.

Jordan put the bracelet around Lily's ankle. "I stole that from the front counter of Mo-net's," he said. Mo-net's was a woman's dress shop in town. Lily took her foot from her mule and held her leg up. She pointed her toes and admired the bracelet. Lily saw herself on the private beach of a Mexican hotel, listening to Spanish ballads on a transistor radio, her toenails painted blue. Whenever she pictured herself in Mexico, doing something like bargaining with fishmongers on a dock or saddling up a burro at a tourist trap, Jordan was nowhere nearby.

Lily said, "I'm not entirely convinced you can even get me to Mexico. First you buy this old car on its last legs . . ." Jordan was a year older than her, but he seemed, sometimes, years younger. The first night they had sex, in her room in the dark, she'd felt almost like she was molesting a boy. She'd sat naked on the bed, waiting as he fell out of his clothes. He held his hands in front of his crotch, embarrassed by the boner that poked at a sad, ratty pair of boxers with a snap-to fly.

"Seems like you could have faith in a guy," Jordan said. "Your sister would have let me drive her south in this car."

Lily held perfectly still. Jordan wouldn't hear her voice or the rustle of her clothing. She wished that his cheap, lazy efforts to piss her off had no effect on her. *Don't move,* she could hear in her own small voice. Once, years before, out in the pasture with Mabel, a bee, its body entirely an ominous black, landed on Mabel's collar and stepped lightly over her throat. "Don't move," Lily said. "Don't frighten it," she said, her eyes wide open. Lily had been both anxious and afraid to see what would happen to Mabel.

Jordan said nothing more, slid from the hood of the car, and got behind the steering wheel. "If you think," Lily shouted back over her shoulder, "that I'm going to fly into some fucking jealous rage every time you mention how close you are to my sister . . ."

"You would just love for me and Mabel to get together," Jordan interrupted, slamming the car door. "Even just once. Even just once for a short nothing kiss."

Lily contemplated, for a moment, life as a girl mass killer, shooting up filling stations from the window of Mrs. Bixby's Monte Carlo on her way south. She could steal the antique Colt her grandmother had placed in a brown paper sack beneath the cash register. The Mexican headlines would all shout out MUERTA, above a photo of Lily with her trousers tucked into the tops of baton boots, just as the deadly Caril Ann had dressed herself. Lily would compose her shocking diaries on the walls of her jail cell, and, using straightened-out safety pins as knitting needles, she'd sew doll dresses from the thread of her unraveled prison-issue socks. She'd send the dresses back to Nebraska, to her niece, the daughter Mabel and Jordan would have had together by then.

"If I confessed to a short nothing kiss with your sister," Jordan went on, leaning slightly out the car's open window, "you'd shut yourself up and just rage for days. Then everything in that house would be about getting Lily's forgiveness. But you know what, Lily? I don't want to kiss Mabel. She's sweet, but I don't want to kiss her."

Lily got in the car next to Jordan and took out her cigarettes. "Poor Mabel," she said, sounding snide, but she meant it some. Lily had found a photo of Mabel and Jordan—Mabel in blue jeans and a tropical-flowered bikini top and Jordan shirtless in a pair of chinos cut off at the knees. The photo was tucked into a small tin box kept in Mabel's underwear drawer. One boring day, Lily had jimmied the box open with the tine of a fork. The photo had been the only thing inside, as if it depicted something secret, though it was Lily who had taken the picture on an old wooden bridge over the Platte. But Lily had spent the rest of that day examining the photo: Jordan's arm around Mabel's waist, his hand resting on her hip; Mabel leaning in toward Jordan, the skin of her shoulder touching the skin of his chest. Lily would look at the photo, look away, then look again. It was Jordan's thumb hooked in Mabel's belt loop that caught Lily's eye each time.

Jordan held out his hand for a Virginia Slim, his mouth already full of nicotine gum. Lily lit one for him, and he smoked as he chewed. Jordan's cheeks were red from the heat, and his hair stuck straight up.

MRS. BIXBY lived in a nursing home and was unlikely to ever notice the car missing from her farm. Though Lily could see nothing in the dark barn, she stepped slowly, ducking the rusted scythes and plowshares she imagined leaning out from the walls. She felt a twitching in the soles of her feet, certain she was about to step on a nail. Jordan, sniffling and coughing, practically wept from allergies, and he tied a bandanna, bandit-like, around his nose and mouth in order to breathe the thick air. They discovered the car parked at the back of the barn and covered by a few patchwork quilts.

Jordan pushed open the back door, and the barn was then noisy with the creaking of the frogs from a nearby irrigation pond. Lily knocked away the quilts and got behind the wheel of the Monte Carlo. Not only were the keys in the ignition, but there was a spare set sitting on the dash. Hidden keys and locked doors, and any fear of thieves, were considered impractical by old people in the country. After a few turns of the ignition and some pumping on the gas pedal, the car finally started, and Jordan followed Lily in the Packard, driving to the antique shop.

Inside, at the bottom of the stairs, Lily put her hand to Jordan's chest. Jordan said, "I want to go up and say good-bye to Mabel."

"No," Lily said, and she picked up a heart-shaped box from a shelf and gave it to him. "Eat this candy and wait for me."

"It's probably a hundred years old," Jordan said, sitting down to try a piece.

Passing through the hallway, Lily looked in on Mabel sleeping still dressed with her lamp still lit. Jordan made an ungodly racket down below, the cash register clanging its bells with his hammer blows as he attempted to bust the thing open and burglarize the shop. The lamplight shone on a pair of scissors in Mabel's hand. "Mabel," Lily said, walking to the side of the bed. "Mabel," she said, though she knew nothing would disturb her short of screaming in her ear or beating her awake with her fists. Lily knew what such deep sleep was like. Like narcoleptics, both Lily and Mabel could drop off in the middle of anything into a swift, undisturbable nap. Time and again, their grandmother had had to carry one or the other of them in from the empty field or the ditch or the back of the car. Mabel was the worst to watch sleep. Her eyes were closed only partway.

Lily picked up the newspaper from the floor and saw that Mabel, before dozing off, had been clipping an article from its back pages. Two very young girls had been left, by their father, to suffocate in a hot car in Georgia. One of the girls had ripped all the hair from her head as she died.

Lily had never heard of anything so ghastly. For years, Lily had tried to ignore the grisly news clippings Mabel had left on her pillow, not wanting to give Mabel the satisfaction of upsetting her. But this story, at this moment, seemed the worst of them all. "Mabel," Lily half shouted. "Mabel." She pushed at Mabel's shoulder. How could Mabel, a girl with a life so disrupted, sleep so soundly? Lily wanted to slap the hell out of her, to scream at her for putting this image in her head—this dead little girl with fistfuls of her own torn-out hair.

Lily lifted the scissors from Mabel's loose grip and took up a handful of Mabel's hair. She wouldn't cut off quite that much, she decided, and she let some of the hair fall from her hand. She then released some more, then more, until all she held were a few strands. Mabel's hair was so fine, so thin, and as soft as a ribbon. Lily set the scissors on the nightstand. She ran her fingers along Mabel's long neck and along the jut of her collarbone. She ran her fingers across her shoulder and down her arm to the very small bones of her wrist. Mabel seemed so slight, so fragile; she could so easily become nothing. Lily could see Mabel, a ten-year-old, concocting their mother's sloe gin and Coke after a terrible fight between their parents. Their mother had packed up Mabel and Lily and taken off to the secondhand shop for a week, refusing their father's phone calls, not consenting to a visit. Each time they made the drink, Lily and Mabel consulted the wrinkled and water-spotted pages of a bartender's manual they'd found on a bookshelf in the shop. They were nervous, and they whispered to each other, careful to measure everything correctly, as if the key to their mother's contentment lay in the drink's perfect rendering. When their mother finally called their father to offer forgiveness, it had seemed to Lily that the very worst was absolutely over.

Lily wanted to cradle the little girls she remembered, to comb down the fine hair on their soft heads. Mabel opened her eyes. "What is it?" she said.

"Why didn't Grandpa and Grandma Rollow take us in?" was all Lily would say. Though her grandparents' backyard at 4214 California was surrounded by a brick wall, Lily could sit in the cleft of a tree and hear the tiniest sounds of other lives lived: the clattering of silverware as a family ate their breakfast at the table; the squeak of a trampoline.

"What? When?"

"Before," Lily said. "Didn't they want us? Why didn't they fight to have us . . . like some people fight over children?"

Mabel yawned and rolled her eyes like the answer was ridiculously simple. "How could they?" she said. "Their son had just killed himself. And don't you remember how we looked? We were pathetic. Your lips were all chapped all the time, and you kept biting the dry skin off them, and then they'd bleed. And I was so skinny and wasn't eating anything. How would you have liked it? Looking at us like that every day?"

Lily sat on the edge of the bed. "There should have been more done for us," she said.

Mabel sat up in bed and gently pushed Lily's hair back behind her ear. She ran her thumb across Lily's cheek, like wiping away tears. *Come to Mexico with us*, Lily was tempted to say at the touch. But Lily had to simply leave, without one single word. Lily would wait for Mabel to go back to sleep so that Mabel would wake in the morning and find Lily gone. She loved Mabel, but someone had to be left behind. Lily looked at the words she'd written on her hand—Lily needed to be alone with her mother and her list of difficult questions.

LILY HAD BEEN SAVING for months to rent an apartment, dropping her tips into a tin she kept beneath her bed. She took the money, and they headed down the interstate. Jordan drove twenty miles without speaking as Lily lay her head against the headrest and watched out the side window. She felt comforted by the squares of light in the distance, the lit-up, yellow windows of farmhouses. But just a few hours from home, and a few hours from the Colorado/Nebraska border, after Lily had slept for miles, a tire of Mrs. Bixby's car blew on an exit ramp.

"Good thing we slowed down," Jordan said, as they sat cockeyed in the Monte Carlo. He'd pulled off the interstate to get gas. "If that thing'd popped when we were going eighty, we might have rolled to Mexico."

It was only after Jordan made this point that Lily panicked. The whole accident had been gentle, forgiving, as if a congregation of angels had slowed the car. Angels or maybe her father—reckless in life, but now watchful.

"I'm not getting out," Lily said as Jordan attempted to change the tire. Outside, it might as well be raining knives. All the newspaper clippings that Mabel had left on Lily's pillow over the years, all the stories of last slipups, retold themselves: a smart man choking on a fish bone, a boy intending to just flatten a penny on a railroad track, a little girl who trusted her father in a river.

7.

WITH A CAN OF RED SPRAY PAINT, Mabel leaned out an upstairs window and wrote the words THIS JUNK SHOP FOR SALE on the side of the house. She ran downstairs and into the front yard to check her work. Though crooked, the words would be fairly visible to the passing cars of I-80 a mile or so away. She kicked off her sneakers and sprayed them red then leaned back to sit in the scoop of the large satellite dish. A speck of a spider made Mabel's ankle itch. "Don't you know who I am?" she said to the spider as she reached down to crush it with her thumb. All the last week, she'd been running into cobwebs and plucking them from her skin and her hair. She'd catch glimpses of the webs, a shimmer of color out the corner of her eye, only too late. Though she was angry at Lily for leaving without telling her (all Mabel had found was a note Jordan had left next to the cash register—a doodle of a twirling-mustached man in poncho and sombrero beneath the words *Off to Mexico* and above *Don't tread on me*), Mabel had been pacing the house, from worry mostly. Lily had always had higher expectations for things; she was bound to be terribly disappointed in their mother.

Mabel nestled up in the dish, and she looked off to a neighboring farm, to Mrs. Maroon planting tulips in the sorghum field. Mrs. Maroon and her husband had decided it wasn't worth the work of planting and harvesting a crop this summer, so she was extending her flower beds; she'd bought six hundred tulip bulbs and a special device for the end of her battery-powered drill that allowed her to dig holes quickly and easily. Mabel worried that Mrs. Maroon had gone a bit wacko from the struggles of the farm, but what a divine madness, she thought. Uncontrolled tulip planting.

Soon, Mabel promised herself, she would actually be glad Lily and Jordan had left, and she wouldn't care if they didn't come back for weeks. She wouldn't sit around and wait for them, and she certainly wouldn't follow them. She would change her life instead. In the help-wanted section of the paper had been an ad for an assistant at the grain elevator for the longer hours of harvest. Mabel had always liked all the nighttime activity of the cold autumn weeks. As a girl, she had frequently sat up at her bedroom window watching the lights of the combines across neighboring fields, listening to the comforting roar of the engines and the rattle of trucks passing on the road after dark.

Mabel lay her head back and considered herself in other incarnations. She thought she might like to do something selfless for a time, like a woman she knew named Betty who looked after things in the Alzheimer's ward of the hospital. Mabel frequently brought Betty whatever Beanies she picked up cheap at flea markets, and they had lunch in the nurse's station, watching the old folks in the lobby through the tall glass windows.

Mabel would miss the shop and her life among the junk. She closed her eyes and pictured the paint-by-numbers and framed hook-a-rugs on the wall and the junk jewelry locked up in its glass case.

Business had improved a bit at the secondhand store after a recent discovery; an antique dealer bought a ratty blanket that had been draped across the top of the upright piano for years. Mabel got eleven bucks for it, which she had thought a great sale considering the blanket was threadbare and riddled with burns. A few weeks later, the local newspaper carried a story trumpeting the dealer's selling of the blanket, an Indian relic of ceremonial purpose, for $50,000. People trickled in then, investigating all the dustiest tchotchkes, scrutinizing every costume jewel and wineglass and cardboard print in gilded plaster frame.

Mabel took advantage of the new interest in the shop by scratching French-sounding names into the paint at the bottom of cheap vases; on the title page of an old copy of *The Sun Also Rises* she wrote FRANCIS—THANKS FOR THE GREAT TIME IN GREAT NECK.—ERNIE; on every porcelain thing marked with "Japan" on the bottom, Mabel stamped "Occupied" above it and quadrupled the price. She even practiced an elaborate trick she learned from an underground antiquing newsletter: she mixed baby powder and automobile paint, then coated an old rocker or an old trunk with the mixture. She'd light the piece and let it burn a minute, to give it the look of something centuries old.

Nobody fell for the more obvious forgeries, but many altered items were sold; people would approach Mabel, fretting over particular pieces of junk, biting their lips, afraid of questioning authenticity and calling attention to the possible great worth. So she never felt guilty about her deceptions because the buyers had come with their own deceptive schemes—a husband and wife would stand whispering over something like the mock authentication papers of a Tiffany lamp knockoff, then decide to quietly pay the low asking price. They all hoped to get their own pictures in the paper praising brilliant thefts, their ability to recognize the rich histories of things broken or torn.

Suddenly Mabel's hands felt lighter, unencumbered, and she realized she was no longer wearing the ring Jordan had slipped onto her finger in The Red Opera House. Where did I take it off? she wondered, and she worried that the ring was lost. If Lily happened to call, Mabel would say, "Tell Jordan I can't find the ring he gave me."

Mabel slid from the satellite dish as Mrs. Cecil, who'd once been the town's undertaker, drove in to the driveway, pulling up next to Starkweather's Packard. Mabel felt embarrassed by the red words on the side of the house. She didn't want to sell the shop; she just wanted to punish Lily and Jordan, wanted to worry them when they returned on the highway, with a bright red sign that announced they'd ruined everything. "Do you still have the extreme unction box?" Mrs. Cecil called to Mabel as she stepped from her car.

"The what?" Mabel said.

"The old box that used to hang on my wall," Mrs. Cecil said. Ever since retiring from the funeral business a year or so before, Mrs. Cecil had been selling Mabel her antiques one by one, only to return a few days later to buy each one back. Mrs. Cecil was a beautifully preserved old woman, the shriveled, spotted skin of her hands the only sign of her great age. She was stately in her pearls and cameos and silver buckles. Her white hair was smoothly upswept, with the palest tint of blue.

Mrs. Cecil had prepared Mabel's father for a closed-casket ceremony, but Mabel had never felt uncomfortable around her. Mrs. Cecil had long been a friend of Mabel's grandmother, and once when she visited years before, Mabel and Lily described to her the funerals they wanted. "Ringlets," Lily had said, circling her fingers all around her head. "And the green velvet dress that doesn't fit me anymore that I wore two Christmases ago." Mabel had wanted to be buried in a rabbit fur coat she'd seen in a JC Penney catalog.

"'This junk shop for sale'?" Mrs. Cecil read aloud.

"Not really," Mabel said, but looking up, she was no longer embarrassed. She decided she liked the crooked letters marking the house. The words might lend her life some mystery, Mabel thought. Everyone who drove by would wonder and worry about all that was going on within the walls. Lily had never liked people to know about the sad details of her life and had told many lies growing up, often claiming her parents were missionaries far away teaching heathens about medicine and God. Mabel, however, had basked in sympathy, speaking often of her father's death and had even invented a sickness for her mother that required her to take the healing waters and vitamin-rich sun of a little town in Mexico. Mabel had at times claimed the sickness to be hereditary, and she had once given her best friend Cindy a list of wishes she was to mail to the Make-A-Wish Foundation in the event of Mabel's decline (*to swim in the ocean with dolphins; to ice skate in Rockefeller Center, New York City*). Though Mabel hadn't told such a lie in years, she sometimes felt this make-believe illness making her sleepy, causing her bones to ache and her teeth to itch.

Mabel followed Mrs. Cecil into the shop and up to a box hung on the wall. It was a shadow box with statuettes of Mary and the crucified Lord, and beneath the figures was a small, hinged reproduction of the Last Supper. "Behind here," Mrs. Cecil said, undoing a hook with her crooked fingers and lowering the picture, "is the Communion plate and a bottle of oil for anointment. I don't even know why I sold it; it's a nice old piece. How much?"

"You can just have it back, Mrs. Cecil."

"Oh no, oh no," she said, taking her checkbook from her handbag and checking the price marked on the side of the box. Mrs. Cecil spilled some coins from her purse, and Mabel bent to pick them up. "Excuse me, sweets, I'm shaky as a leaf." It must be nerve-racking, Mabel thought, to live among the families of those you'd dressed and undressed and cleaned and powdered and sewn up for burial. She was probably frequently haunted by the ghosts of the living, confronted by the widows from past funerals. People could easily come to think her funeral home—its walls painted always the same pale blue, its rugs the same weave, its slipcovers the same flowered print—a monument to all their old grief.

Mrs. Cecil wrote a check, then lifted the extreme unction box from the wall. She carried it in her arms to the front door, stopped a moment, then stepped out. She then stepped back in. "When did you say Lily would be back?" she said.

"I don't know," Mabel said. "I haven't heard anything."

Mrs. Cecil looked around the house, avoiding Mabel's eyes. The many rings on all her fingers tapped against the box in her arms. "When I drove up just now and saw what you'd painted on the side of the house, I knew I had to finally talk to you girls. To tell you before you move away." She swallowed, and she licked her dry lips. "To tell you about what I took." She put the box down and walked slowly to Mabel.

As Mrs. Cecil took something from her purse, something wrapped in a handkerchief, Mabel longed for her to reveal something stark and awful. Skin from Mabel's father's skinned-up elbow, the lobe of his ear, the corner of his mouth. This time she'd believe absolutely, not like with the suicide note. This time she wouldn't doubt for a second, she promised herself. "I've had this in my purse every time I was here," Mrs. Cecil said. "But I could never bring myself to give it back." Mrs. Cecil held out her open hand and lifted away the edges of the handkerchief. She held, not something horrible, but a small plastic panther. The toy's purple paint had chipped from months of play. Mabel recognized it at the touch.

"It's been in the back of my mind for years," Mrs. Cecil said, pinching at the beads of her necklace.

Mabel studied the panther. Her father had ordered a small bag full of plastic jungle animals from an ad in the *TV Guide*—a bag of panthers and lions and elephants. She and Lily had not cared well for the panther in the few years they'd had it. It had been stepped on and gnawed on and caught in the vacuum cleaner.

Mrs. Cecil wiped her handkerchief at the sweat of her forehead and neck. "I didn't think much about it at first," she said, her voice a high crack. "I have to believe that any funeral director would have done the same. We have to be very particular about how we prepare the caskets for burial. Before the funeral, your mother had wanted to just look at your father in his suit. I advised her against it, even though I had done . . . well, a rather, if I do say so myself, a rather good job of repairing the head . . . as best as it really could be repaired, really. But that's what she wanted, so I lifted the lid for her to look. Though Lily couldn't see in, she was standing right there, and I saw her reach up and drop something inside. I didn't think much about it. I just waited until your mother and Lily stepped back out of the room, and I simply removed it. That plastic panther. I simply removed it and put it in a drawer. Then after the service, and the burial, after all the dirt had been filled in, I realized what I had done. Lily had wanted your father buried with that toy, and I had prevented that from happening. After all these years, Mabel, I haven't stopped thinking about it. Some days it seemed like that panther was alive in the drawer, pacing back and forth." Mrs. Cecil cleared her throat and picked up the extreme unction box. "I hope Lily can forgive me," she said.

"Of course we can," Mabel mumbled, her mind caught on the image of her father dead in his box, his head patched. Mabel had not seen his dead body, and no one before had ever described it. She and Lily had been in the country as their mother alone selected a suit, hopefully the blue one he loved.

He'd worn the slick-looking suit backstage at Mabel's second-grade production of "Little Red Riding Hood." Mabel was only Hedgehog No. 2 in an old bristly brown costume that smelled of mice, but he brought her a present anyway, a tiny box of candied violets he'd special-ordered from a wedding cake baker. He'd decked Lily out in Mabel's cast-off green velvet Christmas dress and had strung silk ribbon through her hair. Mabel's mother stayed at home to nurse another terrible headache.

"Those headaches kick the hell out of her," Mabel's father told Mabel's pretty teacher as she last-minute stitched the ripped lining of Little Red's cape. "They're very decapitating."

"Debilitating," Miss Wyle corrected with a wink, and Mabel's father blushed and chuckled and stroked his stubbly chin.

"Yeah, that," he said, then offered to finish fixing the cape so that she could dash off to look for the lost bottle of wine for Little Red's basket. The other children, so overwhelmed by the sight of this tall, strange man as he sat in a low, tiny chair, all gathered round to watch him simply sew. "I know that dirty mug," he said, nodding at a boy who lived down the hall from them in the apartment building. "That face needs to meet the business end of a washcloth." The kids all yucked it up at that, and Mabel sat on the floor beside her father, her head resting against his leg, so that everyone knew he belonged to her.

He helped Little Red on with her cape and called her "Suzy-Q" even though her name was Bethany. Then he shook her hand and wished her luck. Mabel could recall nothing about the show itself, but afterward her father invited Miss Wyle out for a cup of coffee. The only place open had been a highway convenience store with a few booths in the back; they all shared a few packages of clearance-shelf carrot cake. The adults had coffee and the girls split a 7-Up. Mabel's father told Miss Wyle about the day Mabel was born, and she reached across to lift his floppy bangs to see the scar on his forehead. Mabel wished her father would marry Miss Wyle. She loved her mother, but she'd always wanted a stepmother too, like other girls had. Stepmothers, she thought, so desperately want love and respect and a place in the family.

After Mrs. Cecil left, Mabel realized she'd been gripping the plastic panther tight in her fist, and now it felt hot, felt like it was throbbing in her hand. Touching it was like touching at a vein on Lily's wrist. The panther had not been Lily's best toy, but Mabel could understand why she had chosen it for their father. The artist had given the cat a wide, comical grin of fanged teeth. The panther burned in Mabel's hand like a talisman, and she couldn't wait to show it to Lily. Lily would fall apart at the sight of this secret offering seemingly exhumed from their father's grave. For even just a moment, Lily was certain to be a broken little girl again, her father's death new in her heart.

8.

WITH THE PLASTIC PANTHER WARM IN her fist, Mabel felt drawn toward Stitch Farm. Years before, Brandi, the Stitch girl, had inhaled too much airplane glue from a paper bag on the night of her junior prom. She now sat in a wheelchair, unable to move, barely able to speak, but with a newfound gift. All the farmers' widows had made pilgrimages to the young woman's weekly sessions, standing in line with buttons in their fists and cufflinks plucked from their husbands' funeral shirts. Mr. Stitch would take the items and press them into his daughter's unfeeling hand, and Brandi would choke out a word or two, a message whispered to her by some voice in an afterlife.

Mabel had always rolled her eyes at Lily, had snapped her gum to show indifference, whenever Lily returned from Stitch Farm dressed in mourning weeds—black blouse, black skirt, her father's wedding band on a chain around her neck.

After every session Lily had plopped shut-mouthed and gloomy into the sofa cushions, drinking store-bought margaritas straight from the bottle. But Mabel wasn't as skeptical as she claimed to be. Lily simply needed her to be faithless and free of ghosts, needed Mabel to be the sensible one.

She placed the plastic panther atop the dash of the Jimmy and drove out toward the highway. As a drop of sweat rolled into her eye and burned there, Mabel remembered sitting on the roof of the porch years before as Lily concentrated on a tattered Ouija board. Lily touched the board and asked a question about their dead father's sadness in life, and the triangle spelled out JOSHUA 10 13. Mabel had pretended to be absorbed in a book but later looked the verse up in her grandmother's Bible. "So the sun stood still and the moon stopped," the passage read. *That's exactly what everything felt like*, Mabel thought now, wiping away sweat with the back of her hand.

As Mabel approached the dirt road turnoff, she slowly passed two young men pushing a stalled pickup. An older man followed them, hunch-shouldered and wiping his neck with a hanky. ROSELEAF RANCH was painted in blue on the faded-to-pink truck. In her rearview mirror, Mabel saw that a boy, about fourteen, oversteered at the wheel. She considered stopping and offering her help, but she figured they'd just laugh at her—four men offered help by a girl.

On the country road, just before the entrance to Stitch Farm, the blossom of a plastic mum flew across Mabel's windshield, a few broken petals catching in a wiper. She then noticed all the artificial flowers and silk greenery in the ditch—bouquets stuck into the ground with wires or tied to fence posts. Banners marked TO MOTHER and FOR MY SON fluttered in the wind, loosened from their wreaths. The farmers' wives no longer decorated the plots at the county graveyard. Instead, they took their flowers here, preferring to believe their loved ones to be not beneath ground but in the light and wind surrounding Stitch Farm.

Mabel had visited her father's grave only once, a month or so after his death, to help her grandmother plant a peony bush. On the drive home after, Mabel declared she would never return to the cemetery, as she picked the graveyard's dirt from beneath her fingernails. She'd hated the tombstone's bland inscription of LOVING SON, FATHER, AND HUSBAND and its ugly gray rose cut into the granite. Now Mabel wished she'd been more devoted, with some simple tradition or ritual of her own. She could have burned a candle one night a year or left a single rose on winter days.

The panther in the front pocket of her blouse, Mabel parked and stepped from the car. As she'd left the shop, she'd taken a garish daisy-print umbrella from the wall to keep the sun from burning her scalp. All the old ladies had warned her that if she ever visited Stitch Farm to drink plenty of water and to eat plenty before; people were forever fainting and swooning there in the summer months.

Mabel opened the umbrella and picked the petals from the windshield wiper, looking out across the farm. The only growth anywhere around was a patch of waist-high wheat, a circling labyrinth cut into the field. TAKE A PEACEFUL WALK AND FIND YOUR CENTER—$5, the sign proclaimed. She watched, amused, as people stumbled, dizzied from the twists of the field.

Mabel recognized an old woman sitting on a rusted tractor plow overgrown with weeds and black-eyed susans—Mrs. Lindley, who raised emu. Mrs. Lindley clutched a black tube of sunblock in her fist: SPF 50. "I'm glad you finally came out to see Brandi Stitch," Mrs. Lindley said. "What'd you bring to show her?"

"Nothing," Mabel said. She wanted to keep the panther mostly unseen, to keep it her own secret for as long as she could. Too many questions about it, too much explanation, might take away its power.

Mrs. Lindley held forth a dime. "I found this in the pocket of one of Mr. Lindley's trousers that I'd boxed up years ago," she said. "Brandi's finally going to be able to reveal it all to me this time, I'm certain. I just have a feeling about it. It's evidence, of some kind, this coin, of an affair that he had a few years before he died. I just know it. This is change back from something he bought for her. A Hallmark card maybe. Maybe violets."

Just a dime, Mabel thought, touching at her pocket, at the panther inside. *How sad.*

A cobblestone walk led Mabel and Mrs. Lindley toward the tin-roof lean-to in the pasture, under which Brandi did all her communing with the dead. A crowd gathered at the fence, many standing up on the slats like at a rodeo. Everyone craned their necks to try to see into the lean-to just yards from the padlocked gate. Shadows stretched and moved across the ground as workers, hidden by the tin wall, prepared for the morning's séance. Mabel could hear country music buzzing from broken speakers. The sun was already beating down, and Mabel held her umbrella above Mrs. Lindley's head. Despite the sun block, Mrs. Lindley's bleach-white skin cooked swiftly to pink.

As Mr. Stitch stepped from around the lean-to, as the people caught their breath with anticipation, Mabel wanted to rush away from the whole event, to once again be a person too serious for Stitch Farm. The man looked silly with a long peacock feather stuck in the band of his straw cowboy hat. Mabel giggled, both nervous and embarrassed, at the feather bristling and fluttering in the wind, strutting, like it was still attached to its bird.

But when Mr. Stitch beckoned the crowd, saying, "Come to Brandi," in a deep and kind voice as he unhitched the fence gate, Mabel stepped forward. His chin was stubbly and gray. No one had ironed his shirt. He'd lost his little girl, basically, and what could be worse?

She dropped a donation into an overflowing kettle as she followed the crowd around the corner of the lean-to. Some cotton-candy–scented candles flickered in jelly jars lined up atop a railroad tie on the ground. Mabel walked along the tin wall; stretched across the front of it was a coiling barbed wire. To the barbs, people had stuck photos, newspaper clippings, wedding invitations, hospital bracelets. People had signed their names to poems and prayers they hadn't written, about serenity and footsteps in the sand. Mabel took from her pocket a clipping she had cut for Lily, an article about a Coney Island amusement park ride spinning off its axis and severing the leg of a woman. She gingerly placed the clipping in the curl of the concertina wire. A woman smiled at Mabel as she tied a frayed hair ribbon to the wire, and Mabel blushed, feeling welcomed into the terrible miseries they were all there to share.

Mr. Stitch pushed Brandi's wheelchair out to the lip of a pickup's open tailgate. Brandi, now a woman of about twenty-five, had to have been sweltering in her raggedy cashmere suit. The suit's skirt showed many snags from the edges of the chair. "That's the suit Sally Jessy gave her for the show they did," Mrs. Lindley whispered to Mabel. Mabel remembered having heard about Brandi's appearance on Sally Jessy. It had to have been five years, or more, before.

Mr. Stitch stood beside Brandi and began without ceremony. He held out his arms, his palms up and open, wiggling his fingers. "Anybody got something?" he asked the crowd. Two women stepped forward, one holding out what looked to be a piece of string. Mr. Stitch took it from her, balled it up, and put it into Brandi's hand. He then leaned over, putting his ear to Brandi's lips, hiding her blank face from everyone. He straightened up and returned the string. "She says, 'A hat,'" he said.

"A hat?" the woman mumbled.

"A hat?" the other woman said.

The crowd waited silently for the women to make some connection. Mabel pictured a straw hat and a colorful scarf. A hat, she whispered, desperate for the women to find their way back to a particular sunny afternoon.

"Oh, yes," the woman with the string finally said. "Oh, oh, yes." She put her hands to her face and cried. "A hat," she sobbed. "Of course. The hat." Her friend took her by the shoulders and directed her back toward the gate.

People stepped forward, one by one, with their bits of cloth and pieces of jewelry and letters bound with ribbon. " 'A flower,' " Mr. Stitch imparted. *A book. A picture. A necktie. A map.* Some merely shrugged and walked away, but most collapsed in heartbreak and tears. The panther felt heavy in Mabel's front pocket, and she could feel its edges pressing into her breast, could feel its tiny claws scratching for purchase. Her heart beat fast with both her belief and her disbelief. She so wanted to fall apart, but she knew that whatever Mr. Stitch told her, whatever words Brandi passed on from beyond a supposed grave, would be meaningless. But she also knew she'd return to Stitch Farm with everything she could find that her father had touched. If Mr. Stitch said the right word in the right way it might work, she thought. I could be haunted too.

With all the shade from the umbrella working to keep pale Mrs. Lindley from sizzling away to nothing, Mabel felt the sun's heat weaken her knees and ankles. She noticed a few people fall slowly to the ground, some with something like a Hallelujah wail, almost gleeful in their pain. Mabel lowered herself to the dirt, then became frightened by all the crazies towering above her, mere footsteps from trampling her. But she was too dizzy to move. "Do you need my sunblock, Mabel?" Mrs. Lindley said, as Mabel pressed both hands to the ground to feel still. She closed her eyes and all the most banal junk of her life swam among the dots of her vision—just spoons and forks, pairs of scissors, shoelaces, pencils, light bulbs. She then saw her mother, her mind lost, on one hectic afternoon with her coat over a flesh-colored slip, frayed lace at her knees. That day, months before her father's suicide, Mabel's mother went from store to store secretly slipping her things from her deep coat pockets onto the shelves in a kind of reverse kleptomania. She left a Hummel among boxes of cough elixir in a drugstore, her wedding ring in a china cup in a department store. In a dress shop, she took a Swiss Army knife from her coat pocket and dropped it into the pocket of a coat on a mannequin. Mabel and Lily ran along behind her, huffing and puffing and tumbling over each other's legs as they struggled to keep up with their mother's quick pace. Lily, frightened, had put her hand in Mabel's pocket.

"Anyone else?" Mr. Stitch said, wiggling his fingers. "Anyone else?" Mabel caught his eye as she took the panther into her fist. *A coffin*, she thought, as if prompting him. *A little girl in her best dress*.

"I've got something," a man shouted, and the crowd, tilting their heads with sad smiles of recognition, parted for him and the others following him. Mabel saw that they were the men who'd been pushing the broken-down truck on the highway.

"Yes," Mr. Stitch said, "come forward, Mr. Roseleaf."

The one young man wore black boots held together with silver duct tape; another wore blue jeans torn at the knees and at the back pockets. The men looked to Mabel like they had just crawled out into the sun after a long afternoon of sleep. This was exactly what she'd hoped to see, she realized, all these little signs of helplessness.

"It's Roseleaf and his boys," Mrs. Lindley told Mabel, as she helped her up from the ground and offered some of the umbrella's shade. "The boys lost their sister in that swimming pool incident. They're out here every week with something."

Mabel now remembered the Roseleaf family, who lived in the next county over, from a newspaper article she clipped for Lily years before. The sister, a girl of about fourteen, swam with one of her brothers. As she dove underwater at the deepest end of the pool, her hand or her foot caught with the suction of the drain, and her brother, unable to loosen her, swam to the surface to shout for help. Her other brothers came out then, and her father and her mother, and all they could offer her was their breath. They took turns swimming to the bottom to hold their lips to the girl's, filling her cheeks. One after the other they dove, carrying air to her, keeping her alive for a while with a graceful, wordlessly devised system. But she died before help arrived.

Mabel had been close to the girl's age at the time. After

first hearing of it, she had tried to experience what it had been like for the girl as she had drowned. She swam to the bottom of the municipal pool and imagined that the girl taught herself to find comfort in the water, in the blur of her hand before her own face, in the veins of sunlight at the floor. It would be something like being inside your own body, pulsing through your own flood of bloodstream. The shouts of her family would have been as soft as the popping of a far distant gun.

Mr. Roseleaf held out a half-eaten candy necklace to Mr. Stitch, who put it into Brandi's fist. The Roseleaf brothers all held hands, standing as close as sisters, as Mr. Stitch listened to Brandi. He straightened up, nervously tugging at his ear and at his chin. He took off his hat and put it back on. He was clearly struggling with his imagination, wanting to offer the Roseleaf family something profound-sounding, something poetic and new. *Oh Christ, just say anything*, Mabel thought.

"A . . ." he said, "a . . . um . . . a starfish . . . a wet starfish . . . in the sand." Mabel liked that, the starfish, and it brought to her mind the soft crashing of the oceans she'd never visited. Mr. Roseleaf wailed and sobbed, but the older brother, with the swift, certain manner of a reasonable man, simply stepped up to the truck to retrieve the candy necklace. Mabel couldn't take her eyes off them and their ragged, dirty clothes and hair that needed cutting. *I can believe in your ghost*, she wanted to whisper to the sweet, lost men, *and you can believe in mine*.

"You know," Mrs. Lindley said as the crowd dispersed, "my cousin's daughter's stepdaughter got the Roseleaf girl's marrow. Or they think so, anyway. That information is kept confidential. They sent a letter to the Roseleafs, through a caseworker, but they never got a response."

"They haven't recovered," Mabel said before following the Roseleafs back to their truck. She watched, in a daze, as the boy got behind the wheel again and as the two older brothers gave the truck a push to get the engine sputtering. *They've lost everything*, she thought. As she memorized the phone number painted on the truck's door, tapping the number out on the back of her teeth with the tip of her tongue, she became determined to know them, and to know all their methods of grief.

9.

AT THE COUNTER OF A TRUCK STOP café, Lily dropped some tiny plastic cups of creamer into her purse. She took out a little clear baggie of milagros and spilled them like a pocketful of fortune-telling runes across the speckled Formica. As she looked out the window, watching Jordan talk to a mechanic in the garage, she rubbed the milagro between her fingers. She put it in her mouth, held it at the tip of her tongue.

As Lily had driven west in the middle of the night, Jordan sleeping deeply in the back, she was afraid the Monte Carlo would pop another tire or fall apart completely. With her hands on the wheel, her foot on the pedal, the car became an extension of her arms and legs, and she could feel the car's damage in her body; every catch of the brakes she could feel in her ankles and knees, and every click in the steering column snapped in her wrist. She had made Jordan stop for some adjustments at the first station they'd found open in the early hours of the morning.

Lily's list of questions for her mother was folded neatly, buried at the bottom of the purse at her feet. With this milagro on her tongue, her eyes closed, she could almost hear her mother's voice damp with tears. She could feel her mother's breath hot in her ear and could see her lips form around words that offered no answers.

Then Lily saw into the past and felt the weight of all those afternoons when her mother lay on the living room sofa with her black hair weaving about the tassels of the pillow. Her mother's sleep had exhausted them all; she always slept in the middle of the room, in the middle of the house, controlling everyone without a single word or look or gesture. So as not to disturb their mother, they stepped lightly, mouthed their conversation, chewed their hard candy with slow, hesitant bites. Her mother's constant sleep had especially exhausted her father, weakening him day by day.

"Are you all by yourself?" a waitress asked with a cluck of concern, her hair an unwashed beehive, tiny wrinkles rimming her bright red lips from years of puffing on cigarettes. She set the coffee in front of Lily. *Where's your mother?* Lily half-expected next. It was a question she'd been asked a lot as a girl, constantly separated from her grandmother and Mabel at the grocery store, the school events, the carnivals. "Where's your mother?" said the strangers, their eyes gentle on hers.

"None of your fucking business," Lily said, then she immediately felt bad for the kindly waitress. She picked up her purse and walked outside and around the corner to the restroom. She felt a twitch in her eyelid. Maybe Mabel, back on the farm, got a piece of gravel in her eye. A talk show on the TV above the café counter had featured two sisters: The one in California got stung in the foot by a mean red ant, and the one in New Jersey couldn't walk for a day from the stabbing pain of it. But Mabel was too dull for psychic connection, Lily concluded. If she wanted to communicate with Mabel, she'd have to call her. But she didn't want Mabel to know that she and Jordan were stranded nowhere near Mexico.

After locking the restroom door, Lily dropped her purse on the sink and rummaged around for her bottle of orange-flavored baby aspirin. The chewable pills always helped to settle her nervous stomach. Lily found the bottle, but inside was only a dark yellow dust.

Lily suddenly missed Mabel terribly and longed for her resourcefulness and her overprotection. She hoped Mabel wasn't mad at her for saying nothing about leaving, and leaving no note. Lily would tell her—and this was partly true—that she'd worried about such words hanging in the air. Something like *I'll be back soon* had too much a ring of final irony, sounded too much like the last line of a girl lost forever. She could see Mabel, years in the future, taking Lily's crumbling good-bye note from the fire-safe box, saying, *But she wasn't back soon.*

On the wall, a vending machine featured novelty condoms, with *YOU LIKE CANDY, LITTLE GIRL* written above the list of flavors: *peppermint stick; blowberry; cream soda; pink lemonade*. Lily, amused for a moment, put her quarter in and turned the crank, hoping for *honeydew*. She got *cherry pop* and opened the package to lick it. It wasn't terrible, though the taste of latex did overwhelm. Lily closed her eyes and comforted herself with thoughts of her room back at the house, of the antique paper valentines she'd pinned up along a long crack in the wall. *Haven't I been desperate to see you again?* she wanted to ask her mother. *Isn't this what I always wanted?*

Lily hoped the Monte Carlo was a wreck. Jordan could take her to some roadside motel, to sheets that smelled daily of fresh detergent, to long baths with the little wrapped-up bars of face soap and tiny bottles of shampoo placed every afternoon at the side of the tub. She wasn't as decided about all this, about this journey, as she had thought. Now that Mabel was nowhere around to be shocked and bothered, Lily didn't feel so defiant. She really did want to see her mother again but only if her mother wanted to be seen. The slightest bit of disappointment on her mother's face, and Lily wouldn't know what to do or say.

Jordan knocked at the door. "Lily?" he called out. "You in there?"

"No," Lily said.

"Don't be mad," he said. "It's not my fault. The mechanic's taking his own sweet time."

Sweet time. Lily thought about sneaking home on foot. But what she really wanted was to go back years, to when her father's death had yet to seem real, when she didn't yet know that her mother would never return. The days before that, when they all lived in the old apartment with its bright yellow walls, seemed too far away to be even believed and longed for. *His own sweet time.*

"Lily," Jordan said softly, "I've got an idea." She could tell he was leaning his head against the other side of the door, his lips close to the crack.

"Can I ask you something?" Lily said. "Did Mabel and me turn out all right? Despite everything, do we seem okay?"

"Well, hell, yeah," Jordan said. "I mean, you guys are a little fucked up, but who the fuck isn't?"

"Lots of people aren't," Lily said, thinking of the commercials she'd been watching on the TV at the counter. Lily resented the ads of daytime television, the false sense of security—the images of women strolling beaches, the housewives dissolving in bubble baths, the mothers in kitchens discussing cleanliness with their daughters. Lily had read about cultures in which the women were exiled from their homes during their periods, sent out into the wilds. Actually, she thought she wouldn't mind living in such a culture—having even a few days a month to drop from society, to go sit in a river and bleed.

"We could leave the Monte Carlo behind, Lily," Jordan said. "You don't have to be in that car anymore." *Jordan's worried,* Lily thought, deeply relieved. *I've worried him.* "The mechanic told me about a bus that goes to Vegas direct. Vegas is out of our way, but we could get married there, if you wanted to."

Lily leaned against the closed door. "Is that how you're

supposed to propose to a girl?" she said, but she felt herself blushing, anxious to accept. If she didn't marry Jordan soon, her destiny might be thrown off by years. She wanted to become a professional clairvoyant, so Las Vegas would be the perfect place to set up shop, to make a living easing guilt and psychic pain, locating missing persons and missing dead. People, she thought, like to have their lives told back to them, like to hear from a stranger who they've been and who they'll be.

"Will you marry me?" Jordan said. Lily thought about how thin Jordan was. Anyone could lift him with one finger and blow him away like an eyelash. But she said yes anyway.

Before leaving the bathroom, she took out a lipstick from her purse and wrote *I'm being held against my will* across the mirror above the sink. She still felt bad about being rude to the waitress. She hoped the woman would find the note and think better of her later.

LILY DECIDED to trust the mechanic when he told her he replaced a this and a that, and that the Monte Carlo, the old workhorse, would outlast them all. The mechanic was a handsome man in his thirties with a gold tooth and one jet-black Superman curl drooping across his forehead. He chewed on a toothpick as he winked and flirted with both Lily and Jordan, and he smelled of a mixture of dime-store aftershave and Bay Rum.

"I should marry *him*," Lily said, driving down the street to a restaurant the mechanic had recommended. Jordan had wanted to go someplace nice to celebrate their engagement. "He doesn't seem like the type to make his girlfriend drive."

"Drop me off at the restaurant, then," Jordan said, pissy. "Go back for him."

"I'm just kidding," Lily said, reaching across to slap his stomach.

"Ouch," Jordan said.

"Pussy." She had been kidding about wanting to marry the mechanic, but there were worst fates.

At the restaurant, Jordan rested his hand, palm up, atop the table as the young waitress took their order. He popped a cough drop into his mouth, knocking it against his teeth, then scratched at the scar, clearly trying to impress the girl. The mechanic had elbowed Jordan in the ribs as he told her about the waitress. "She's our low-rent Lolita," he'd muttered. "She'll fuck your brains out for a forty-ounce and a handful of Bazooka. No fucking shit, man." It pissed Lily off a little that Jordan had laughed at that, in that half cough, half cackle that men make when they're making fun of slutty girls. But, she'd thought, he might just be laughing to be polite.

The waitress, long and gawky with flyaway blond hair kinked from braids, seemed to be squinting at Jordan's wrist. Jordan always went slick with charm whenever a girl noticed his scar. "A breakfast steak and a cup of joe, precious," he told her. "And if you really want me make me happy, you'll toss some grilled onions on the plate."

The waitress smiled only a little, leaving the table as

quickly as she could. "What's it like to think about suicide?" Lily said, lighting a cigarette.

"It's on your mind all the time," he said, smiling with lips closed. "It's like having a crush on a mean girl." Despite Jordan's scarred wrist, he didn't understand anything, Lily thought, about the possibility of death.

She thought about how easy it would be to pick up the steak knife at her elbow and poke him, just a little. "You know," she whispered, her finger tapping the knife, "I could give you another scar. But I won't because you'd probably welcome it, probably want the scar so there would be something you could show off, so everyone could know how crazy your wife was. I can just see you in some bar with some other woman. 'I was just sitting there sucking on a cough drop,' you'd say." She thought about how little it would take to blind him if she wanted to. It seemed a miracle that most people made it through life with their eyes still in their heads, considering all the carelessness in the world.

"Marrying you off to that mechanic is sounding better by the minute," Jordan said.

"Let me read your fortune," she said, taking the palmistry book from her purse. She held the book open with one hand and, with her other, ran the burning coal of her cigarette just above the lines of his palm. "Not good," Lily said, though she didn't fully understand the book. The instructions seemed to be poorly translated from a foreign language. "Your liver line is bleeding into your kidney line." Jordan kept his palm open, even as Lily put the cigarette closer and closer to his skin.

They looked into each other's eyes, each of them waiting for the other to flinch.

"Ow," Jordan finally said, squealing like a girl, snapping his hand back. "Fuck you." He left the table and walked to the restroom. The blue ink on Lily's hand, the questions for her mother she'd jotted down, had not yet washed all away. The words up her arm now looked like fading bruises, needle tracks. She regretted mentioning the mechanic. She looked forward to marrying Jordan, to their locking themselves up in a motel's honeymoon suite, to exist there like vacationers during a tropical storm. They could mix martinis in the plastic ice bucket and rent soft-porn pay-per-view. Or they could watch the Vegas tourist channel all night, happy to be missing it all.

Lily noticed an elderly couple across the restaurant watching her. There may have been some worry, some pinch of concern, on the faces of the couple, she thought. They may have sensed a doomed, short-lived matrimony for Lily and Jordan, but Lily didn't mind their judgment. She even felt a little flattered—they must have recognized her maturity, she thought. They wondered how such a smart woman would cope with such a gangly, childish, near-miscreant for a husband.

Jordan returned to the table, but didn't sit down. He reached into the pocket of his tight jeans. "Let's do this like we're supposed to," he said, holding up an antique ring. "Will you marry me?" The licorice smell of his cough drop reminded her of winter.

"Yes," she said. When Jordan took her hand, Lily pictured

herself in bed with him years and years in the future, and she imagined waking and finding he'd died in his sleep. What would it be like to wake without him that morning, after years of getting up together and sharing a simple breakfast in a familiar nook? How painful would it be? She saw her old-lady's hand touching the cold skin of Jordan's cheek. There was so much she never wanted to learn about herself.

10.

MABEL HAD CONSIDERED A DISGUISE for watching Mr. Roseleaf and his sons. In the antique shop, a collection of wigs and wiglets were pinned to faceless Styrofoam heads lined up on a vanity. Mabel and Lily used to wear the wigs when they played "Divorcées Having Pepsi at Three," a soap opera they invented. Lily always wore the Ginny, a butch brunette with uneven bangs, and Mabel wore the Sheila, a permed and almost-orange red.

But Mabel decided there was no need for a costume—the Roseleafs never seemed to notice anyone. She put on the cherry-print dress Lily had worn the other night. It was too big for Mabel, so she wore a beaded sweater over her shoulders. The nights were cooling off.

She drove to the corner café of the little town of Willow, the next town over from Bonnevilla. The café was a place everybody called Closed Mondays because those were the only words left on the faded sign. Inside, the Roseleafs had shoehorned themselves into a tiny booth in the corner. Wyatt, the oldest son, a man in his mid-twenties, unscrewed the bulb of the lamp above the table, and the family sat unspeaking and huddled together, watching their dark reflections in their cups of decaf. One brother poured Sugar Twin into another brother's cup. One dabbed up the other's spilled coffee with the cuff of his own sleeve. Another scratched the father's back, and the father straightened another's collar.

Old Mrs. Lindley had seemed to know a lot about the Roseleafs: Wyatt's father had been a fan of western novels, and had named his boys after Wyatt Earp, Jesse James, and Buffalo Bill Cody. The sister's name—Callie—came from Calamity Jane. But all that the boys' mother had ever read was the Bible and her subscription to a monthly devotional called *Portals of Prayer*. A few years after Callie's death, Mrs. Roseleaf left her family to work at an orphanage in Nicaragua.

At a table across the café, Mabel wrapped up her french fries in a square of newspaper, paid her bill, and left Closed Mondays. As she drove into the country, she steered with one hand and, with the other, held open a brochure for an eye bank.

Cornea transplants, Mabel read, *have a success rate of more than 90 percent. Each year, over 35,000 cornea transplants are performed.*

Mabel had once read in the newspaper of a young man who befriended the mother of the girl whose eyes he'd received. They'd become quite close and spent holidays together. Mabel wasn't proud of the story she was inventing for herself, but she longed to sit in the rooms of the Roseleaf family, having so simply woven her way into the intricacies of their misery. "I received your sister's eyes," Mabel rehearsed out loud in the car. There was something poetic about the sound of it, something welcome. It was almost like something out of an old movie, a women's weepie, Mabel thought.

But she only knew what Mrs. Lindley had told her at Stitch Farm. The Roseleafs might not have donated Callie's eyes or any other organs. In their religious fervor, they could have refused donation afraid that Callie would be risen again when the world ended, blinded and with no heart beating in her chest. And why shouldn't they, Mabel realized, why shouldn't the family of a dead child deny all beggars everything? All life taken from a child, and the world wants to take more? *No*, Mabel would have said to all the thousands of people dying without Callie's heart and liver and kidneys, burying her daughter complete and deep in the ground.

Mabel drove for twenty minutes before reaching the broken fences surrounding the Roseleaf Ranch. After parking next to the tall brick wall at the backyard, she got out and stood on the hood to see over. Despite the great heat of that summer, the swimming pool sat empty. The cracked floor of the pool was littered with beer cans and the broken twigs of an old tree shading the yard. Mabel kicked off her clunky sandals and hitched up her dress to crawl over the wall, then dropped down into the shallow end of the pool. She followed the sloping floor toward the drain that had trapped Callie Roseleaf. Among the leaves and the mulch were tiny pieces of colorful, burned paper, red and yellow and green. She picked up a piece and realized it was the popped husk of a firecracker.

At the deep end of the pool were childlike paintings of fish. Mabel walked to the side and wiped some dirt away with the palm of her hand. Each weathered fish had been signed by one of the Roseleaf children. Callie's fish was pink with little blue bubbles of air leaving its lips and forming into the shape of a heart.

Cody had painted a simple, child-like curlicue of a fish. Jesse's fish had fangs and spiky fins. Wyatt's fish wore a derby hat and smoked a pipe. Mabel brushed away more dirt and saw that this little school followed DAD—a Poseidon with long beard and triton—and MOM—a redheaded mermaid in a clamshell bra. Mabel realized that Callie, trapped by the drain, would have looked at these paintings as she waited for her next breath of air from one of her brothers. She would have comforted herself with memories of the day they painted the fish—the whole family standing in the empty pool with their brushes and wearing their button-up shirts back-to-front as smocks.

Mabel walked over to the drain. She reached her hands above her head and looked up to where the surface of water would have waved and broke and trapped the bolts of sunlight. She closed her eyes and saw the bubbles of air rolling off the back of one brother, then another, then another, as they dove toward her, then back up again, then back down again. One pressed his lips to hers, and she took his hot breath in her cold mouth. She touched his cheek, maybe, and maybe his throat; maybe she flicked her tongue in his mouth, just for a taste. Then with all his breath sucked into her lungs, she released him. She was the tragic heroine of a backyard water ballet, the littlest mermaid trapped by her fin, or maybe it was nothing like that at all. Maybe she scratched and clawed them as they tried to leave her, pulling hard at their arms and their kicking legs. Maybe the Roseleaf family nursed their cuts and bruises for weeks after Callie's death.

Mabel took Lily's plastic panther from her pocket. Without much thought, she leaned down and dropped the panther through the cracked drain cover. It was a symbolic gesture, Mabel decided, of some sort or other. She squatted and looked in, and she could still see the panther's bright red open mouth. As she stuck her finger in, to knock the panther farther down, she was startled by the thought that she might never see Lily and Jordan again. They'd love to live a life in secret, Mabel knew, taking an apartment at the edge of a dismal town, blowing their low wages on pickle cards and crime novels. Lily would cherish the power of withholding her existence from Mabel and all the others who missed her. Jordan would just go along with it, thinking Lily loved him more for the effort.

Mabel pinched at her naked finger, almost feeling the antique ring Jordan had put on her hand in the opera house. She closed her eyes, and she could feel the press of his lips so surely that she wondered if he kissed Lily just then somewhere in Mexico.

Shouts and the crashing of something heavy breaking in the house interrupted Mabel's thoughts, and she ran up to the shallow end of the pool. She kept hunched low, crouching lower and lower as the floor inclined. At the end, she squatted, poking her head up over the edge. She could see through the glass patio doors. The Roseleafs had returned, and Wyatt yelled at Jesse while their father and brother rushed upstairs to get out of the way. Wyatt was too angry to be understood, his voice cracking with tears and his words running together. He grabbed Jesse by the front of his camouflage T-shirt and screamed into his face, then shoved him into a chair. He shouted some more, waving his arms, slapping a farm cap from Jesse's head. Finally, Jesse, convulsing with tears of his own, lunged for Wyatt, and they fell back into a sideboard that rattled with silver tea things.

Mabel could no longer see the men when they dropped to the floor, but she could hear all the thump and rumble, and she could see the glass of the patio doors shiver with the fight. She wondered if she should intervene; brothers fought to the death, she imagined.

But in only minutes Wyatt stood from the floor, the fight apparently finished, and he helped Jesse up. Jesse put his fingers to a cut on Wyatt's forehead, but Wyatt slapped Jesse's hand away. Jesse shrugged and went up some stairs.

When Wyatt looked directly at Mabel, she dropped down low and held her breath, hoping he'd only seen his own reflection in the glass. She wished for some wide-lensed sunglasses and the Beret, a feathered, ash-blond wig from the shop. She heard the patio door slide open and the scratch of Wyatt's boots as he dragged his feet, sluggish, across the tile.

Though Mabel sat clutching her knees, her eyes shut tight, she knew Wyatt stood above her at the edge of the pool. She could feel his cool shadow across her hot face. "I know who you are," he said. Mabel didn't answer, and he said it again, and he kicked at some pebbles that fell against her back.

She stood up, brushing dirt from her dress, pulling a few pebbles from her ponytail. *Who am I?* she almost said.

"You're the girl who's been following us," Wyatt said. "You were at Stitch Farm and at Closed Mondays the last few evenings. You've made me curious." A drop of blood rolled down past his eye, and he smiled, unnoticing. He looked so innocent, pressing at a bruise on his forearm, his mussed hair rooster-tailing, that Mabel didn't worry about being caught. Even the fight, now that it was over, seemed somehow sweet-intentioned.

"You're bleeding," she said.

"We haven't had too many girls sneak into the pool since we've kept it empty." He winked at Mabel.

"Do you have a first-aid kit?" Mabel said.

"I don't know," he said.

Mabel took the handkerchief she'd wrapped the panther in and held it up to him.

"I really don't want to bleed on it," he said, even as he took it from her and dabbed it at his forehead. Mabel climbed from the pool, and Wyatt led her to a bathroom with a tall cabinet that spilled over with salves and unguents, suppressants and lozenges, and Band-Aids for wounds of every shape and size. Mabel lowered the toilet lid for Wyatt to sit, and she grabbed some rubbing alcohol and a handful of cotton balls. After she cleaned Wyatt's forehead, she applied a butterfly bandage then bit at a roll of gauze to tear off a square. Though Mabel had always been the fragile one, it had been Lily who'd always required care and pharmaceuticals. As far back as Mabel could remember she'd doctored Lily with the long-expired remedies in her grandmother's medicine chest. Mabel had even been known to coax Lily up trees and beneath hedges of thorns, just to have a new wound to explore. "What were you guys fighting about?" Mabel said.

"Jesse's joining the army or the navy or whatever . . . one of those. He just told us tonight at dinner. We came right back here so I could beat the hell out of him." When Mabel didn't respond, Wyatt said, "You don't understand Jesse. Last year, he joined a cult for four months. We found him in a terrible beard, eating tuna fish out of the can. Before that, for a few months, he was a skinhead."

Mabel held her hands to both sides of Wyatt's face as she pressed the surgical tape against the skin of his forehead. Her knees touched Wyatt's. Wyatt seemed to want to be babied, his eyes closed, his hands folded in his lap. Mabel fantasized a deeper wound, Wyatt bloodied and dizzy, and Mabel leading him to collapse against a sofa. She imagined holding a warm rag to his throat and whispering something comforting in his ear until help arrived.

Distracted, Mabel accidentally pressed a fingernail sharp against Wyatt's cut, and Wyatt jumped, knocking over a half-empty beer bottle sitting at the edge of the tub. The bottle broke on the floor.

"Don't move an inch," Wyatt said, bending down to pluck the pieces of glass from the puddle of swill. The trickle of beer touched at her toes.

As Wyatt picked up the glass, Mabel looked in the bathroom mirror, leaning in close, widening her eyes to see all the tiny blood-red veins. She watched a pupil grow larger like a drop of ink on paper. She imagined Callie looking in this same mirror and running her fingers over her cheeks and lips and the edges of her eyes and wondering what she'd look like when she was older.

Mabel decided to tell her lie. She'd been telling it to Wyatt, in her mind, over and over, all day. Each time she told him, he reacted by taking her hand, thanking her for her bravery. Then he'd kiss at the tear on her cheek.

"I was nearly blind in my left eye when I was a little girl," Mabel said. Near-blindness was a stark reality in her life, something she was entitled to. Her own sister, after all, without her glasses, could hardly see the hand in front of her face. "A warped cornea," she said. "Would you believe me if I told you that they gave me a new cornea, and that it came from your sister? That the woman at the eye bank made a mistake and told me where it had come from, even though it's confidential information? And that's how I knew, and that's why I've been following you? Would you believe that?" The lie spilled out too rapidly to be believed, she thought, but she saw Wyatt's hands shake as he threw away the broken glass. She held very still and waited. He held his fingers to the side of his jaw, pressing, as if trying to locate a toothache.

"Did you hear me?" Mabel said, in a whisper too soft to be heard. "Would you believe such a thing?"

"Go away," Wyatt said. "Please go away." But then he grabbed hold of her ankle. "Wait," he said, though she hadn't taken a step. He looked up at her. "Why would you lie about something like that?"

"I don't know," Mabel said, truly uncertain of the answer. With just his one question, Mabel was ready to give up the pretending. In a way, she was relieved to be so quickly found out. Wyatt would lead her to the door, speaking softly but sternly, the way people spoke to people crazy and sad, assuring her no hard feelings but *Please don't come around again*. Mabel would go home and write a simple note of apology. She'd blame her lie on her fucked-up upbringing—*Mabel and Lily have had no fetching up*, she'd heard more than once from the old farmers' wives.

But Wyatt had merely been thinking out loud, had asked, *Why would you lie?* when he had meant *No one would tell such a lie*. Meant *So I have to believe you*. "If you'd written a letter," Wyatt said, "we wouldn't have written back. Never in a million years. It would have been too hard to see a girl with Callie's eyes."

"Just one eye," Mabel said.

"What?"

"Just the one eye," she said. "I just have the one cornea." It was important to Mabel to establish this. It made the lie only a half lie in her thinking.

As Wyatt stared at her, Mabel wondered if he was looking for some evidence of surgery—delicate scars where the pieces of shattered color had been stitched together. She felt conscious of her every blink and began to blink too much. She felt a lash sticking and put her finger to the corner of her eye. Wyatt squinted and flinched as if it were his own eye she touched.

"Let's sneak out the back door," Wyatt said at the sound of someone on the stairs. He took Mabel's hand. "Dad made a special appointment with Mr. Stitch. He wants to go practically all the time anymore, every day. But I don't really believe in any of that. Brandi Stitch doesn't talk to the dead. She's nothing more than a fraud."

A fraud. Though it was something no one should want to be, Mabel didn't mind the sound of it. I'm nothing more than a fraud, she told herself.

Wyatt led Mabel outside and past the pool and down a slope of land to a tiny playhouse. The playhouse had a patchy roof of heart-shaped shingles, and the one last shutter dangled loose on its hinge above a short thicket of mulberry bushes. The birds had picked the bushes clean, and their black shit streaked the chipped whitewash of the walls. One note of whimsy remained of the house—the pipe chimney of the roof had a knot in its middle.

Wyatt told her to duck to enter as he opened a short Dutch door. Snow White accepted a poisoned apple through such a door, the top half open, the bottom half closed, and the pumpkin eater's wife was kept very well behind one.

The playhouse was dark inside, so Wyatt reached up and screwed in tighter a bare bulb. When the light filled the room, Mabel saw the wallpaper still bright with a pattern of cherries and oranges and lemons like on the wheels of slot machines. Wyatt said, "Callie had wanted wallpaper like Willy Wonka's; of course they don't make candy wallpaper, but Dad did find some with those scratch and sniff pieces. So, do you recognize the place?" and he kind of laughed and winked, then pointed to his eye when Mabel didn't get it. "Seeing with Callie's sight?"

"No," Mabel said, though she didn't mean to be rude. Much of the fruit on the wall had been scratched dull by Callie's fingernail, but Mabel found a grape bunch near the ceiling still a slick purple. Mabel scratched lightly at it, releasing its sugar-wine scent, and she closed her eyes. *No*, she thought, *I don't recognize anything about any of this at all.*

Wyatt opened the door of a cardboard oven. Inside were cassette tapes, and he popped one into a tape player on the windowsill. Mabel didn't recognize the song or the singer's voice, but the sad, lazy twang of the music made her think of women in cowboy hats and turquoise rings.

"I just come out here to hide and drink," he said, picking up a half-empty bottle of wine stoppered with a broken cork. "Callie used to ask me to come in and join her tea party, to sit with her dolls, but I never did." He held the bottle, but didn't open it. "She'd make little invitations for me, but the most I ever did was stand outside the window here every now and again and take a little pretend sip from a cup."

Mabel held a miniature china sugar bowl in the palm of her hand and studied the intricacies of the tiny, pink painted roses. For a moment, she envied Callie her short sweet life, her brother at her window, her dolls in their chairs.

"I had always wanted a playhouse like this," Mabel said.

"We built it from a kit," Wyatt said. He produced a pear from somewhere and sliced off a piece for her. Mabel ate it in one bite, then plucked a seed from her tongue. People like Wyatt were the only people she should be around, Mabel concluded—people just sick about missed tea parties and other lost minutes.

Cries of Wyatt's name came down from up the hill. *Wyyyy-aaaaat*, in the slow deep voice of fathers calling across farms for children. Wyatt, still holding the bottle, grabbed Mabel's hand again. His thumbnail was black, maybe from a hammer blow, and he wore boots that looked to be made of snake. They ran from the playhouse, across the ranch and across neighboring fields and pastures, over creek beds and through patches of tall wild grass. When Mabel realized she should have her shoes, they'd gone too far to go back. Wyatt took Mabel deep into a cornfield, which was like dipping into a cave, the air too thin, too wet to breathe. Sunlight fell against the leaves of the stalks, casting green shadows, and the various music of crickets and grasshoppers made it hard to hear anything else. *Stay out of the fields*, Mabel's grandmother had once warned years before. *You can't find your way out when the corn's above your head. You get all turned around, and you don't know your left from your right*. The day after hearing that, Mabel walked into a neighboring field, stepping only a few rows in. Her intention was not to get lost but to catch a glimpse of where lost was. But she hadn't anticipated that the leaves would be as sharp as the edges of paper and would leave tiny, tattling red marks on her face and arms and legs. When her grandmother saw her, she burst into tears in the kitchen, her hands shaking as she attempted to tie up a pot roast with string. "I should never warn you girls about anything," she cried. "You hear about it, then you try it out."

11.

MABEL CAUGHT HER DRESS ON A barb of a fence as they trespassed onto some pastureland. Buckthorn, she'd thought, identifying the wire; many farmers had been selling off their collections of snippets of barbed wire fence, and Mabel had got to know all the different kinds and their value—brotherton, twist oval, necktie, arrow plate. Mabel examined the long rip. "Caught on the devil's hat-band," she said, as Wyatt stuck his fingertip through to touch the skin of her leg.

Wyatt led Mabel up the short, grassy side of what seemed a hill but wasn't a hill at all; it was an earth-covered storage shed, an abandoned bunker that had stored the bombs and munitions manufactured at a nearby factory during World War II. Like the other sheds lined up for miles across the government land, it was covered on three sides by dirt and grass and patches of heather and wild daisy. Mabel looked out at row upon row of the deceptive mounds of earth like sacred tombs lined up in mystery formation. With her feet bare, she could feel the hollowness of the hill beneath her, could feel the wind working, circling through the empty shelter.

The sun had set and the air was cool, but Mabel took off the beaded sweater as she sat in the grass. Wyatt handed Mabel the sweet white wine for a swig.

" 'And the fragrance of your breath like apples,' " he recited quietly. " 'It goes down smoothly for my beloved,' " he said, " 'flowing gently through the lips of those who fall asleep.' "

"Let's hear some more," Mabel said, wanting more of his solemn, preacher's voice. She lay back in the grass and watched dark clouds move too quickly, like in time-lapse, across the sky. They needed the rain; they all said it.

" 'Sustain me with raisin cakes,' " he continued, the Song of Solomon, Mabel thought, recalling her father's love for the more musical passages of the Bible. " 'Refresh me with apples, because I am lovesick.' " Wyatt could have been a minister, Mabel thought. He was handsome in a way that wasn't at all frightening, and his voice, something like a stage whisper, you could feel in your spine. He could convince you of the existence of all sorts of impossible things.

"There was a group of religious girls at school," Mabel said, "who used to invite me and my sister, Lily, to church things—ice cream socials and church fairs. I remember a ventriloquist. When he opened his dummy's mouth for it to talk, you could see the wire at the back of its throat. I couldn't keep from looking at the wire, though it was awful and I could practically feel it when I swallowed." Mabel swallowed, pained just at the thought of it. Wyatt swallowed too, touching a finger to his throat, but he asked her nothing more about this sister named Lily, or about any other detail of Mabel's life. This was fine with Mabel; she didn't mind, for a time, being a girl whose only misfortune had been one bad eye.

Wyatt lay down near Mabel. He closed his eyes, and Mabel watched him rest. She pictured him as a boy, his chest smooth and flat, his legs chicken-like in a pair of swimming trunks.

Mabel studied Wyatt, his sideburns too long and crookedly cut, and a long, fallen eyelash on his cheek. His hair curled at the back of his neck, and there were a few too-early grays in the black. "You need a haircut," she said, though he didn't really. It just seemed a thing you said to a guy you liked.

"Haircuts aren't until Sunday," he said.

"Sunday?" she said.

"Ever since we were little kids, Dad has given us haircuts on the last Sunday afternoon of every month. He used to pull the TV into the kitchen because they showed old movies on the educational channel. We boys liked the foreign ones because sometimes they'd show some titty. *Contempt*," he sighed, "Brigitte Bardot in a bathtub." Wyatt smiled and winked and thumped his hand against his chest like a fast heartbeat.

Mabel reached over and lifted the cross from his chest, running her thumb along the tiny silver Christ in agony.

"I bought that at that little gift shop at Stitch Farm," Wyatt said. "I just liked it." She sat up on one arm and knew that her shoulder strap had slipped, showing off her bra some, but she left it. Wyatt pushed the strap back up. *If I kissed you*, Mabel imagined him saying to her, *I wouldn't want you to think it was because I was thinking of my sister or anything like that. Because that would be weird.* Wyatt closed his eyes again to the few raindrops that fell in his face, and he licked some drops from his lips. The early evening became as pitch dark as night. In the split seconds that lightning struck and lit the sky, all the dark clouds lit up. "Sinister," Wyatt said, pointing to the electricity. "Did somebody tell you how Callie died? Is that why you were in our pool today?"

"You and your family nearly saved her life," Mabel said.

Wyatt smiled and winked. "Or just made her death longer," he said, joking in that way people do to show they're scrappy in the face of terrible loss.

WHEN THEY RETURNED to the Roseleaf house, all the lights inside were out, and Mabel saw the dot of a candle flame at the window. She and Wyatt ran in to the front room, both of them soaked, and Mr. Roseleaf tossed them each a beach towel. "They think they spotted a funnel," he said with a smile, a transistor radio held at his ear.

"This is Mabel, this is Tyrone Roseleaf," was all Wyatt said in the way of introduction.

"What're you kids drinking tonight?" Mr. Roseleaf said.

"One old-fashioned," Wyatt said. "Cocktail?" he said to Mabel.

"I dunno," Mabel said, reaching back to twist the rain out of her ponytail. "What's good?"

"Anything that doesn't need water," Mr. Roseleaf said. "No pump without electricity."

"I'll have a vodka gimlet," Mabel said, just because she liked the sound of it. It seemed what Ingrid Bergman would drink in a Hitchcock movie.

"You heard the girl, Daddy," Wyatt said, taking Mabel by the hand and rushing her down the shag-carpeted basement steps. Jesse and Cody were on the floor, drinking highballs and playing poker with sticks of gum by flashlight. Cody tossed back a shot of something clear and shuddered as if from hearing fingernails on a blackboard. "Put away the nudie cards, boys," Wyatt said. "A lady's present." Cody slapped at Wyatt's ankle as Wyatt took Mabel close for a dance. Their clothes very wet, Mabel got a chill and stifled a sneeze. "On rainy days," Wyatt said, nodding toward an old Bakelite battery-operated, "that little AM station in Bonnevilla goes all Louis Prima, between the weather alerts." Wyatt rocked his shoulders, singing along to "Banana Split for My Baby," and held his hand low on Mabel's back. Mr. Roseleaf stepped up to them with a tray of drinks. A penlight in his mouth gave the bourbon a red glow from the maraschino cherry.

The first sip of the gimlet sent a tingle clear to Mabel's fingertips. Another sip, and she had to have a seat in a corner recliner. She realized she hadn't eaten anything all day but a few fries at Closed Mondays. She wished she'd asked for the old-fashioned, so at least she'd have the cherry to eat.

Wyatt and Mr. Roseleaf sat down to the game of poker, Wyatt next to Jesse like they hadn't had the knock-down, drag-out just a few hours before. Mabel refused the invitation to join them; instead she kicked her feet up in the recliner and watched the boys fancy-shuffle the cards and announce each game with a sharp's side-of-the-mouth mutter: Devil's Weed and Double-Humped Deuces Wild; Pretty Maids in a Row with Diamond Ear Bobs; The Queen's Been Raped and All the Knaves Are Guilty.

Later in the evening, the rain stopped, the wind no longer shaking the glass of the narrow basement window. Mabel even thought she saw some light beneath the door at the top of the basement steps. But the Roseleafs ignored the electricity and continued with their happy hour in the dark. Mabel pinched her nose and downed another glass of vodka, determined to learn to love the booze, so she'd be invited down in future storms.

Back at her own house, she'd often dragged Lily into a closet for disaster preparation. Mabel, a stubborn little girl, had never believed that hurricanes would not touch them so many miles from the shore and that earthquakes only happened on fault lines. A box in the closet contained only necessities: cans of Spaghetti-Os and Spam and Vienna sausages, a crystal radio Mabel had built from a paper kit, a book, dated 1909, on wolf and coyote trapping. *If you are using small animals for bait*, Mabel had read aloud, by candlelight, to Lily in the closet, *such as jack rabbits, cotton-tails, prairie dogs, badgers, or sage hens, use the whole animal, if your method will allow of it, and do not skin the bait, as that will make the coyote or wolf suspicious*.

Mabel drifted off to sleep, and she dreamed that Lily tried to kill her with ladybugs, lettuce, and gasoline. When she woke, the moon was out from behind the shreds of clouds. All the Roseleafs were asleep on the basement floor. Mabel wanted to wake them and continue with their party in this cramped basement room. The night reminded her of the scene in *Some Like It Hot*, when all the band members toss a party in Jack Lemmon's sleeping compartment on the train, mixing their drinks in a hot-water bottle. Mabel had seen the movie as a little girl and had always longed to be invited to an impromptu midnight party in a tiny space.

Mabel's dress was still wet and cold, so she took it off and crawled, in her bra and underwear, to Wyatt. She put her nose to his throat to smell his aftershave. She noticed the dry skin on his neck, peeling from a sunburn, and she peeled a piece away. Lily burned every summer and her dry skin flaked off in sheets. She let Mabel peel at the dead skin as she sat in her bikini, her back bare. The simple act had so satisfied Mabel that she'd often picked Lily's skin sore.

Mabel put her ear to Wyatt's lips to try to hear what he mumbled in his sleep. When he stopped talking, she held her mouth above his, stealing the taste of candied cherries and whiskey. She breathed in his sleeping breath, breath that had helped keep his sister alive for a while as she perished at the very bottom of the pool.

Mabel was afraid for that day when Wyatt learned of her deception. She thought of those mothers she read about in a magazine—women who secretly poisoned and sickened their children in order to bask in the attention of doctors and nurses when they carried their babies into hospitals. The mothers were said to have "Munchausen syndrome by proxy," a name Mabel loved. Mabel realized she must have a similar syndrome, in her lying to the Roseleafs. And this kind of Munchausen-by-proxy had been blossoming for years—there'd been a girl in grade school Mabel had loved, a wrinkled, bald-headed child with a disease that aged her prematurely by decades. Progeria, another wonderful name, suggesting some island principality. Mabel had longed for a touch of progeria, only to be closer to that little girl who wore a beret crocheted with bluebirds and birdhouses.

12.

LILY AND JORDAN TOOK THE MONTE Carlo to Las Vegas after all, the old car making the ten-hour trip without incident. At a rest-stop tourist booth along the way, they'd picked up a brochure about Vegas weddings; as Jordan drove into town, Lily navigated from a map on the back of the brochure, directing them to the Marriage License Bureau—it was late, but the office stayed open until midnight. Both cranky from the long drive, Lily and Jordan stood in the crowded lobby of the bureau and filled out the papers with the golf pencils they'd been given. They were married just down the street, ten minutes later, in a five-minute ceremony.

In their motel that night, both exhausted, Lily lay in bed with the pillow balled up at the back of her neck to keep her wedding-day ringlets fresh. After the ceremony, she'd had her hair done in a salon in the El Cortez. Her wild ringlets were still gathered up and speared with stems of baby's breath. Unable to sleep, she flipped open and closed the lid to the antique ring Jordan had placed on her finger.

She sat up and turned on the light to watch Jordan asleep beside her. He lay entirely still, and Lily could touch the pulse point of his wrist, his bottom lip, his eyelash, without waking him. The skin of his arms and his cheeks had creases from the wrinkled sheets and pillowcase. When Jordan had first started spending nights with Lily, he'd been restless, sitting up late reading romance novels Lily's mother had left behind. If he'd fallen asleep, anything would wake him—the click on of the refrigerator or a cricket on the windowsill. But after a few months of living among Lily and Mabel, he seemed to catch their habit for deep sleeping.

Lily had been studying how to read the bumps of people's heads, and she ran her fingers over Jordan's as he slept. She closed her eyes and saw herself as an old woman in an old dress, sitting deep in Jordan's future in a shaded chair. She had a brief vision of Jordan patiently unknotting a knot in the lace of her boot.

Lily wouldn't leave him after all, she decided. She was tempted to wake him up to tell him that—to tell him that she'd thought of leaving him, and that she'd changed her mind watching him sleep so soundly. It might worry him, might instill some proper fear, to know that his wife made important decisions in the middle of the night without him. The nights might not pass so peacefully for him then.

Lily lay back and closed her eyes and, to relax, promised

herself that she didn't have to go any farther south. She'd send her mother a picture postcard of the feathery showgirls of Vegas. "We got this close," Lily would write, with nothing else but her name.

I just don't think it's worth it, Lily thought, then she said it softly, out loud, hoping to hear a certainty in her own voice. But her mouth was dry and her voice cracked and she sounded like a child. Lily touched at her hair, at the sprig of baby's breath breaking to pieces. She wanted to call Mabel, to wake her in the night. Lily wouldn't have to say anything. *Don't tell me*, Mabel would say, scolding but concerned. *Let me guess*. It was what Mabel always said when Lily called crying over some boyfriend from a phone booth on the street corner or from a friend's house in the middle of the night. *Don't tell me, let me guess*. Lily closed her eyes and tried to sleep thinking of Mabel's voice, running the words over and over through her mind. *Don't tell me Don't tell me Don't tell me*.

Jordan spoke, startling Lily, and for a second she thought he might be talking in his sleep. His eyes closed, he said, "You've never been this far from home before, have you?"

"Neither have you," Lily said.

"Yeah, I have." He rolled over on his side and put his arm around Lily's waist. "When Mom and Dad were trying to save their lousy marriage, when I was a kid, we took a family trip to stay in some bungalow on some beach in Virginia. There was a big storm and the windows broke. Dad cut the hell out of his hands cleaning up the glass. Things got better for a while, though, because me and Mom looked after him, bandaged him up, poured him his Jack and Coke. Kept those cheap stogies of his lit."

What the fuck do you know about anything? Lily thought, tears in her eyes. You've had a beautiful life.

"I want a divorce," she whispered, but he'd already fallen back to sleep or was pretending to sleep. If only he knew how to do something useful, like change the oil in a car. "I want a divorce," she said again, crying but looking forward to returning home, when everything was over. She'd rent her own little place in town, hang up pictures torn from magazines, cook small meals on a tiny stove. She could go work with the secretaries at the grain office, the ladies addicted to Diet Coke and books on self-improvement. Lily fell asleep imagining slow hours of painting her nails dull colors, watching the clock, plotting a better life.

WHEN SHE WOKE again a few hours later, Lily picked up her suitcase still packed and left Jordan in bed. It was still the middle of the night. *I'm not abandoning him,* she told herself. She just didn't want her mother to see him yet, to see him scarred and scrawny, before Lily had had a chance to make any kind of impression. She hung the DO NOT DISTURB/NO MOLESTE sign on the doorknob, then walked across the quiet lot to the Monte Carlo. At least the car was running better now, she thought.

Driving alone through the dark, along a highway that wound around mountains and hills, frightened Lily, but the terrible route distracted her from thoughts of her mother. When sunlight began to glow over the tops of the hills, when all she had left of the drive was the security of interstate, and when the radio began with its live, cheerful early-morning chatter, only then did Lily feel her stomach turning with nerves.

South of Tucson, the miles were marked off in kilometers, giving her only a vague sense of how long she'd been driving. Lily imagined her mother on this same stretch of highway leaving behind her children and her husband in his grave for the land of bandits and earthquakes and miles of bad road.

As she neared the border, she saw SAINT ADELAIDE'S WINERY—NEXT EXIT on a small billboard. She reached into her bag for the wine label her mother had sent weeks before; PRODUCED AND BOTTLED BY SAINT ADELAIDE'S WINERY it read in small print beneath a drawing of a mug shot of a terrifically mustached cowboy, a bullet hole in the upturned brim of his hat. Above him, it read OUTLAW ROSÉ. Lily held the label against her cheek, closed her eyes a second, and saw her mother and a man slow dancing knee-deep in crushed grape.

In her stomach and in her head, Lily felt that dizzy, dip-in-the-road nausea, and she drove onto the exit ramp with hesitation. For so long she'd been picturing her mother in her southwestern life, just a washed-out rendering, all seen as if looking through a piece of green glass. But with just one slight turn in the road, all the familiar images were thrown into confusion.

A dark purple variety of prickly pear was suddenly thick

along the road. She passed a beat-up bus parked at the side of the interstate, where a group of women prisoners in bright yellow jumpsuits cut brush with scythes. A guard stood nearby, the butt of a rifle resting against his hip. Up ahead was the whitewashed façade of Saint Adelaide's, a bell in its short tower, and Lily became afraid again. Not for herself, really, but for her mother. A simple tap on the shoulder on an ordinary day, and you're faced with your little girl nowhere she should be.

Lily pulled into the cul-de-sac of the winery and parked next to a dry, tiled fountain. Her 'do had collapsed from the wind of the drive, and she tried to repair it. She took from her purse a polyester scarf she'd bought from a souvenir shop (STOLEN FROM MUSTANG RANCH written across it), then put on some lipstick and clipped some sunshades onto her thick glasses. Lily licked her fingertips and adjusted a curl at her forehead. She looked a bit like a broke Vegas rat, and she liked it.

Impossible questions rolled through her mind too quickly to jot down. *Do you ever wake horrified in the middle of the night with worry for your children? Do you see us when you look in the mirror? Did you hate us for needing you?*

On the thick oak doors of the entryway was a CLOSED/CERRADO sign, above a listing of the hours. The tasting room would be open in a few minutes. Lily lit a cigarette and recalled a sexy border town in one of the first movies she ever saw. All the movies that played the Mazda were at least ten years old, some twenty, some thirty or forty, movies that were cheap for the theater to rent. Many of them were troubled-youth movies of the 1950s and '60s—girls in tight pedal pushers snapping their gum and hating all the people who had got anything from life. The movie Lily remembered starred Jack Lord, her dad's favorite actor. A woman rode in Jack Lord's convertible, and her long stringy hair blew all around. This small, skinny woman had terrified Lily, the way she'd first come on the screen, stepping around the junk of a gas station, lurking around the corners. The sting and rattle of the music or her slinkiness or maybe even the way she chewed her gum suggested something terrible to Lily. But she never did find out if the woman did anything to Jack Lord. Lily's dad rested his arm at the back of her seat, and she leaned her head back and fell asleep. When she woke up, she was slung over her dad's shoulder, the theater lobby upside down. Lily was scared for a second, thought she was falling, then relaxed. She put her fingers in the back belt loops of her dad's jeans and pressed her cheek against the soft cotton of his shirt.

Lily brushed at her leg when she realized the coal of her cigarette had fallen and burned a hole in her dress. *This is close enough*, Lily thought, and she started the car and put it into reverse. She hit the gas and longed to drive in reverse all the way back to Nebraska. It would be satisfying to be the one to put the distance between herself and her mother, to watch the miles of road grow between them. But Lily slammed on the brakes when she heard a thump and caught sight of a motorcycle darting out of her way.

"I'm sorry," Lily said, opening the car door. "Did I hit you?" The woman on the motorcycle wore a leather jacket and thin chains, a bandanna tied at her forehead.

"You couldn't hit me if you tried," the woman said. She smiled and turned off her bike. "I just pounded my fist against your trunk to startle you."

Lily was fascinated by the woman's long dirty braid with twigs caught in it. *Are you my mother*? she thought, in the words of an old storybook she'd read in the school library, a book about a bird, knocked from its nest, questioning all the creatures it came across. But Lily knew this wasn't her mother. Her mother had blue eyes and no birthmark on her neck.

"You been here before?" the woman said. "Me and some friends are camping out just down the road. The sisters bottle a great port. It's like thirty bucks a pop but well worth it. The nuns do a swift business. They make money hand over fist, but not just at this. Margaret Bridget trades stock on the Internet."

The doors were opened then by an old woman in stiff, new, bright blue jeans and a T-shirt embroidered with roses. A woman in a khaki skirt and plaid blouse pulled a large terra-cotta pot around to prop open the door, then sprayed the cactus in the pot with a mister. Lily had hoped for, at least, familiar nuns, women in white habits maybe speckled with the splash of red wine. The nuns gestured hello, and the motorcycle woman said she needed to buy a corkscrew. "Though I've opened bottles in the desert without a corkscrew before," she said, mostly to Lily. "You wrap the bottle tight in a towel and slam it against a rock . . . pushes the cork out good enough to get at."

Lily stepped into the tasting room and up to a row of oak barrels and wrought iron stools. It was too dark inside to see with the sunshades, so Lily took them from her glasses and paid two dollars for the tasting. The wines listed on the chalkboard had cutesy, desert-theme names, like "Roadrunner Riesling" and "Wild Coyote Chardonnay." She could use a drink, awfully, even something as slight as cartoony tourist wine. But, "Anyone under twenty-one," the nun said, singsong, "can only taste our non-alcoholics."

Lily didn't argue or present her fake ID. She just nodded and tapped her knuckle on the barrel top. She couldn't stomach the thought of even the most meaningless lie. It will be all gut-wrenching truth from here on out, she declared to herself. She'd demand confession and clarity, a nearly unhealthy honesty, from everyone in her life, even passing strangers. She wanted the truth right now from the nuns and the motorcycle woman, wanted to hear their every dirty thought and secret unspoken cruelty.

As the motorcycle woman paid for her little bottle of port, Lily took her mother's recent photograph from her purse. "Have you seen this woman?" she said, a line she'd heard in movies hundreds of times but had never before had the chance to say.

"Of course," the nun said, though the photo was a bit out of focus. "It's Fiona."

Say it again, Lily wanted to say.

"You're her daughter," the motorcycle woman said so suddenly, so sharply, it sounded like an accusation.

"What?" Lily said, but all three women were staring at her, unsmiling, studying her face. They were looking for her mother, or the lack of her mother, in her features and her gestures. Lily felt blood running from her nose, flowing to her lip.

"Oh, sweetheart," the motorcycle woman said, pulling a handkerchief from her back pocket. Lily thought only her sister carried handkerchiefs. Mabel had collected many of them from within the antique shop and had laundered them and kept them in the top drawer of her vanity with pillows of cinnamon sachet. They made Mabel sneeze when she held them to her nose.

Lily licked some of the blood from her lip and felt the blood thick in her throat. The motorcycle woman held the hanky to Lily's face with one hand and held the back of her head with the other, as if administering chloroform.

"Let me go get your mother," one nun said. "She's just in the back."

"No," Lily said and asked for a restroom. In the restroom around a corner, at the sink, she took her glasses off and set them in an empty soap dish. She leaned her head back and pinched the bridge of her nose, the way the school nurse had once advised her after a fistfight with a pansy-ass girl hitter. The bleeding stopped after a minute or two, and Lily washed the blood from her face and took off the headscarf. She undid the pins of her hair and shook some of the curls out a bit, letting her hair fall to her shoulders. Her left nostril was now dark and swollen with clotted blood.

"Your mother's going to love seeing you," the nun said when Lily stepped from the bathroom. All the women were smiling with lots of teeth, trying to look like they didn't notice her warmed-over-deathness.

The nun in the skirt put her arm through Lily's and led her toward a door in the back of the tasting room. They walked outside to a small shed near the rows of circling vine. Lily felt queasy from the sun suddenly in her eyes, and she thought a public vomiting would be just the thing to follow a nosebleed. She bit her lip and pinched the skin of her arm to distract her from her stomachache.

Inside the shed, she saw her mother's shadow cast by the heavy sunlight in the room. Her mother was hidden by bamboo racks covered with bunches of grapes laid out to dry. Lily caught a glimpse of her gloved hand, a glint of light on a garden shear, the collar of her denim shirt. Something very pretty played on the radio, a song in Spanish. "Fiona," the nun said, taking her arm from Lily's and turning back toward the door to leave. Lily wanted the nun to stay, to introduce them, to talk with them, to rub Lily's back, to stroke her hair, to hold her hand.

Lily hadn't been certain what to expect; her mother had sent photos over the years, but she was always blurry in them and poorly lit. She'd once sent a faulty Polaroid that hadn't developed; it had arrived still a chemical swirl of blue and purple and green—she apparently hadn't even waited for the picture to develop before dropping it into the envelope.

Her mother stepped from around the corner of the racks, a not-old woman, but a woman far from the lost young thing Lily had been picturing for years. Like the motorcycle woman, she wore her dark hair pulled back in a long braid, loose strands framing her face. "Yes, dear?" she said, her head tilted.

In that "Yes, dear?" Lily heard a pang of hope, a little expectation, something that suggested that her mother wanted this young woman standing before her to be someone belonging to her.

"I'm Lily," Lily said. Then, "Lily Rollow."

Her mother's smile dropped, her chin quivered, then her smile came back again. "Lily," she said. "Oh, Lily," she said. "Of course, you're Lily. I'd know you anywhere. How could I not? You look just like him. You look exactly like your father." She dissolved into tears then, there, across the room. She held one gloved hand to her face, the other at her hip, and she cried alone. Lily kept her distance, somehow comforted by the lack of her mother's welcoming embrace or kiss on the cheek. Who else in the world would she greet like this? she thought, watching her mother come apart. Nobody else, she thought. Just me and my sister.

"I'm sorry," her mother said, wiping her tears with a towel she'd had tucked into the waist of her chinos. "You just look so much like your father." Lily didn't say anything about how she didn't look anything at all like her father and that of course she'd recognize her because they'd been sending school pictures for years.

"So where's Madeline?" Fiona said. "Didn't Madeline come?" It took Lily a second to remember that Madeline was Mabel's real name.

"She didn't come. And she goes by Mabel now," she said, feeling possessive of her sister's choices.

"Oh, yes," she said. She rolled her eyes and put her hands on her hips in a motherly gesture stolen from a sitcom, like *Oh, yes. Oh, how well I know that wacky Madeline*. "The name I gave her wasn't good enough."

When her mother looked at her again, she furrowed her brow and squinted. "Lily, your nose is bleeding," she said, just as Lily felt the blood wet again at her lip.

"Oh, *fuck*," Lily said.

"Don't say that word," her mother said, coming to her with the towel. Lily didn't mind the gentle scolding. *What else?* she wanted to say. *What other words don't you want to hear*?

After putting the towel in Lily's hand and moving Lily's hand to hold the towel to her nose, Fiona touched her cheek. Lily felt the many rings on her fingers and the rough skin of her hands. Fiona pushed the hair from Lily's forehead and pressed her palm there like feeling for a fever. She then stepped back and took a whole look, and Lily felt too fat standing there in front of her mother who shared Mabel's frailty.

Fiona pointed at the new burn hole in Lily's dress. "You

smoke cigarettes," she said. "I wish you girls wouldn't smoke. You know, other people can smell it, the smoke, really strongly, on you. You don't really know that when you're a smoker. And, I mean, I don't mean to be critical, it's just that I used to be a heavy smoker too, not so long ago, so I know a little something about it. You know, while you're here, over in Nogales, you should get some of that nicotine gum or nicotine patches or something. Everything like that's real cheap down here. Any prescription, really. I don't know if you, you know, if you have medicines that you . . ."

"No," Lily said.

"That's good," her mother said, sighing with what sounded like great relief. They stood not speaking for a moment. Lily was terrified that her mother might suggest cheap diet pills, some black market concoction unavailable in the United States. "Anyway, I've been expecting you, really," Fiona said. "I wished it, really. Thought you two might have come looking for your mother some time ago."

Lily only smiled politely, but her mother kept looking at her, nodding, seemingly waiting for some excuse. Lily thought of what Mabel had said the night Lily told her she was going to Mexico. *What were we supposed to do?* Mabel had said. *Crawl across the desert with our little plastic suitcases?* It infuriated Lily, this idea that she and Mabel were somehow, in any way, responsible for the many years apart from their mother. *You stink like smoke*, her mother says. *What drugs do you take? Why didn't you come sooner?* "What the fuck's that supposed to mean?" Lily found herself saying. "You expected us some years ago? We were supposed to come for *you?* That doesn't seem at all backwards to you?"

Fiona held one hand at her own throat with worry. "Please watch your language, Lily, or . . ." Fiona started, but didn't finish.

"*Or?* Or what? What? 'Or I'll ask you to leave'?" Lily said. "Could that have possibly been what you were about to say to me? Were you going to ask me to leave? Was my ffff . . ." She stopped herself, but started again, "ffffucking whore of a . . . of a piece-of-shit . . . cunt mother going to ask me to fucking leave?"

Her mother's entire lack of response, the way she didn't even take her eyes away from Lily, as if she'd long been prepared for Lily to be crude and foul and insulting, made her feel sick to her stomach again. Lily held the blood-spotted towel up to cover her face. I'm so fucked-up, she thought. Lily wished to be felled by a sudden crying jag, but she was much too exhausted.

"Lily," her mother said, softly. She held her hands gently at Lily's elbows. "Lily, listen to me," but she didn't say anything else. After a long moment, Fiona took the towel from Lily and cleaned up Lily's face. "We haven't been together five minutes, and there's already been tears and blood."

"This isn't me," Lily said. "I don't know why I'm being like this. I didn't come all this way to call you terrible names." How, Lily wondered, on God's green earth, do you apologize to your mother for calling her a piece-of-shit cunt? "I mean, back at home, I'm constantly the one who defends you to

Mabel. We have these fights about . . . about how you must feel and about how things must have been for you. Where you're concerned, I've always been, you know, understanding." She felt guilty for speaking poorly of Mabel, but just now it felt like a gesture of kindness to her mother.

Fiona dabbed a bit more at Lily's bloody nose. "It's so dry down here," she said. She tucked the towel back into the waist of her pants and took Lily's arm. "I'm just down the road," she said, walking with Lily to the door.

Outside, Fiona pointed toward her back-road bungalow, a small, square red house in an enclave of other small red houses in the middle of nowhere. Fiona had had many addresses over the years, but Lily had always imagined her in the same house of dark rooms, looking exactly as she had the day she left. Now all the details she'd conjured in her mind as she'd read her mother's letters—the painted-white writing table and the grandmotherly lamp with a ruffled pink shade—would be replaced with her true surroundings. Lily would miss that house she'd pictured for so long.

"Saint Adelaide," Fiona said, as she and Lily walked through the shade cast by the nun's clusters of vine, "was a blind leper, who was paralyzed and had visions of people released from purgatory because of her suffering." Lily smiled, feeling rubbed raw from all the complaining. Fiona told Lily about the rattlesnake that sometimes lived coiled beneath the air conditioner of the tasting room, and the family of javelina pigs that lost too many of its babies to bobcats.

"I hate to have to tell you this," Fiona said, and Lily's heart jumped. Lily was anxious to hear anything that her mother hated to have to tell her. But all Fiona said was "You're beginning to really burn. You have such a fair complexion."

Lily and Fiona passed unstung beneath a blossoming tree that swarmed thick with bees. Lily could feel the hectic, threatening buzz shivering in the hair on her neck. She and her mother didn't talk about the particulars of their lives. Lily didn't mention Jordan or her Las Vegas nuptials, and Fiona didn't speak of her many fiancés and ended engagements. For just a moment, there seemed something completely perfect about it all, like the quiet, slow afternoons Lily had fantasized that she'd someday have with her mother—an afternoon uneventful, both Lily and her mother so familiar with each other that they were without much to say.

IN FRONT OF THE HOUSE, Fiona broke off a paddle of prickly pear cactus. "For soup," she explained. "Tastes like green bean." Near the porch, a hummingbird nearly brushed Lily's ear in its beeline for a feeder of red-dyed sugar water. "The hummingbirds are treacherous certain times of the year," Fiona said. "But they're good luck, I think."

The porch was crowded by a long sofa piled on with boxes of weathered paperbacks. The plants in all the pots had long since burned dry, and a string of dried chile peppers hung alongside the door. Leaning against the sofa were metal road signs warning DO NOT ENTER WHEN FLOODED and FALLING ROCKS.

Fiona instructed Lily in how to cut the cactus paddle down to its limp, bright green insides, then went to her bedroom and closed the door. As Lily sliced the skin away, repeatedly pricking her fingers on the cactus needles, she could hear her mother on the phone. She closed her eyes and listened, trying to catch a stray word here and there, but everything she heard sounded foreign. Her mother was speaking Spanish. Lily put down the knife and studied the many snapshots on the refrigerator door. Though Lily and Mabel had always sent wallet-sized portraits of them taken annually in the school lunchroom, in front of a swirling blue backdrop, none were among these pictures of strangers. There were also a few postcards tacked up, notes from friends on vacations around the world. One photo showed Fiona with her arm around a dark-skinned, dark-haired girl about Lily's age. They both wore coats, their hair blown by wind, ocean waves frothing and foaming behind them. *Why did I come here?* Lily thought, wishing she could keep her mother in that dark, lonely room that she'd imagined for so long.

Lily put her sore, scratched fingertips in her mouth as she pressed her forehead against the kitchen window, feeling homesick. Looking past the bungalows as the sun set behind them, she tried to conjure up Jordan in Starkweather's Packard kicking up dust and coming to her rescue. He'd take her from her mother and they'd spend the night driving the unpaved roads of Mexico and drinking worm-at-the-bottom mescal. Once they were good and lost in the desert, he'd sing to her, loudly, to get the coyotes to howling, playing all the wrong notes on his guitar.

Lily's stomach hurt with hunger. "Mom," she said softly, hesitantly, realizing it was the first time she'd called her mother that, called her mother anything but a piece-of-shit cunt, since arriving. "Mom," she said a little louder, and "Mom" again, louder still. But her mother stayed in her room.

Lily poured herself some raspberry-flavored wine and then stepped out onto the porch, exhausted from the hours of travel and the thoughts of her mother's other life. After only a few sips of the wine as the sun dropped away, Lily fell asleep on the sofa. She woke when she felt a sharp pinch at her arm. "I haven't been able to wake you," her mother said, tears in her eyes, her hand rubbing her throat. "I always hated the way you girls slept so deep." Lily rubbed at the spot of skin still stinging and pink from her mother's fingers. The pink quickly faded, and Lily pinched her arm again to bring it back.

Fiona had undone the braid from her hair, and Lily thought she looked beautiful and years younger. The tears in her mother's eyes, the catch in her voice, made Lily worry, and the worry made her angry. She didn't come all this way to offer her mother comforting words.

"You were on the phone for so long," Lily said.

Fiona sat on the porch step, her back to Lily, and she began to run a brush through her long hair. "It was the daughter of an old friend of mine," Fiona said. "Ana. Always in crisis. She's in a bad, bad marriage. He hits her, I know he does, but she won't admit it." She pulled hair from the brush, then released the strands into the hot breeze. "You think *you're* unhappy," she said.

Lily started to say something, to somehow defend her own unhappiness. *I just walked out on my husband,* she almost said, *a man who loves me so much.* But instead she said, "I never said I was unhappy." She picked up her wineglass and blew at the tiny fruit flies that had collected on the rim. "If you were so certain that your daughters would show up some day," she said, "wouldn't a person have something to say to them? Some excuse? Even a weak one would be nice."

"I'm sure it would be nice," Fiona said, with what sounded like sympathy.

Lily leaned over, reaching across to tuck the faded tag of Fiona's blouse back into the collar. She's gone forever, Lily thought, watching her mother look out and across the moonlit desert. *When she left, she left for good.*

"You know," Fiona said, "you hear about some mothers who drown their babies or suffocate them. Everybody loves to read about loco mothers leaving their babies in dumpsters or on buses."

"I guess I should be glad you didn't do anything like that," Lily said, meaning it, sort of, as a joke. Her mother glanced sharply back, startling Lily.

"I never hurt you girls," Fiona said, pointing her finger at Lily, her voice shaking. "I may have swatted you a few times, but that's it. But I never really hurt you . . . you know, not in any terrible way. You know I didn't."

For just a moment, moved by her mother's minute of passion, Lily was tempted to sit on the porch step with her, put her arm around her, tell her everything was perfectly fine.

But then Lily leaned forward, feeling both cautious and cruel. "The first thing I forgot about you was the sound of your voice," she whispered. "A few months after you stopped calling us. Then I started forgetting other things that Mabel could remember. I forgot the red slippers you used to wear and how they slapped against your heels as you walked. And there's some night I can't remember, one wedding anniversary when we all went out for fried fish and cake, I guess, and you gave us sips of your beer. And when I was little, I thought 'Oh, that's why she hasn't come back. She's not coming back, because she knows I'm forgetting about her.' "

Fiona sighed, looking down to tear distractedly at a loose thread in the stitch of her canvas shoe. Finally, she stood from the steps and sat beside Lily on the sofa. "I *never* thought I'd be gone for so long," Fiona said. "Not for a minute did I think that. My intentions were always to come back for you girls, I swear it."

Lily rested her leg against her mother's and looked toward the vineyard, hoping for her father's young ghost to stumble in from the dark, to come sit with them. Lily had always asked for what he had left in his lunch bucket—a partly eaten apple, a spoonful of cold tomato soup from his Thermos. She closed her eyes and her tongue burned with the memory of the taste of the toothpicks he soaked in cinnamon extract.

"What should I say, Lily?" Fiona said, some desperation in her voice. "What do you need to hear?"

Lily looked at her open hand, but all the ink had worn off. "I don't know," she said, running her finger along the lines of her palm. "You could tell me that you think about us. That you've always thought about us as much as we've thought about you. That you've worried constantly."

Fiona put her arm around Lily and her head on her shoulder. When she spoke, she sounded as if she hadn't slept for days. "That's what I'll say then," she said. "I've worried constantly. Go back and tell Mabel that I've worried constantly."

Lily nearly believed her. Her breathing rose and fell with her mother's slow, restful breaths. If they sat there awhile longer, her mother might, like a child, drift off to sleep against her. Mabel and I could have taken such good care of her, Lily thought.

13.

CALLIE, THE DROWNED SISTER, CAME dripping into the Roseleaf basement in the middle of the night after the storm. Feathers dropped from her waterlogged angel wings, and her skin was pale and pruney from too long in the pool. She got down on the basement floor and pressed her lips against Mabel's, and Mabel smelled the stink of swimming-pool chemicals in Callie's hair and swimsuit, and she choked on the water Callie forced into her throat. Everything went black for Mabel, and hours later, just before morning, opening just one eye, she saw Mr. Roseleaf kneeling at her side. He held Mabel's hand in his—such a sweet sight that she almost drifted off again to dream of it. Then she realized he'd unlatched her bracelet, a silver piece with cheap yellow stones and was taking it from her wrist. "Oh," he said, caught in his theft, and he gently placed her hand back at her side. Mabel sat up and stretched and saw all the Roseleaf boys standing above her, watching her. Jesse held out a convenience-store lemon Danish, and Cody handed her a Thermos lid of hot coffee. Mabel, starved, devoured the Danish and burned her tongue drinking too quickly. She was too hungry and disoriented to worry about being only in her bra and panties.

"I told them about you," Wyatt said, "and about Callie's eye." He squatted down beside her and redid the clasp of her bracelet. "We didn't want to wake you. They just wanted something of yours to take to Brandi Stitch."

"I thought you didn't believe in her," Mabel whispered. "She's nothing more than a fraud, you said."

"I just want to know what she'd say," he whispered back. "Just out of curiosity. Just to hear what she'd come up with. Why don't you come with us? Let us take you there? To see her?"

"I can't go like this," Mabel said, picking up her dress. "It's all wrinkly and torn."

"Wear something from out of here," Mr. Roseleaf said, taking from a closet a box marked SALVATION ARMY. "Some of these clothes might fit you."

A bird in a puddle flapped water from its feathers, brushing its wings against the basement window, and the fluttering worked up Mabel's spine. Callie's angel had tried to suffocate her in the night. Mabel shut her eyes, shook off the chill, and tried to remember the nightmare more clearly. What had Callie come for? To pluck out Mabel's eyes to wear in her own empty sockets, likely.

Mabel rummaged through the box, pricking her fingers on an unfinished Butterick dress project, the tissue pattern still pinned to flowery material. She unearthed a pair of jellies, a jean skirt with an appliqué butterfly, and a T-shirt that said SUSHI ICHIBAN, a restaurant in Omaha, above a cartoon of a little Japanese girl in a too-big kimono. The T-shirt was a bit tight but it fit. With the girl's shirt warm against her skin, she regretted lying to these men who were so terribly weak, so much weaker than she'd ever been. Why hadn't she just walked up to them that day at Stitch Farm and said, "I've lost someone too"?

It was raining again, and the Roseleafs had all piled into the front of the pickup. Mabel crawled in over Wyatt's knees. She had to practically sit on Jesse's lap, Jesse's shoulder in her back, Wyatt's elbow in her ribs. Cody sat on his father's legs, his own legs up on the dashboard, his head against the roof. Wyatt drove rough down the rutted driveway, knocking all their heads together with each bump. Whenever Wyatt turned a corner, the iron spinner on the steering wheel cracked Mabel on the knee. She remembered a scene from a Marx Brothers movie—a ship's small stateroom filling with the brothers, the engineer, the engineer's assistant, the steward, the manicurist, the maids, and others, until they all spilled out the door.

"Aren't we going to Closed Mondays first?" Mabel said. "For some decaf? For some toast?" The Roseleafs all looked at each other, puzzled, as if they weren't even aware of their own routines.

"That was Callie's T-shirt," Jesse said with a sigh, poking a finger at Mabel's belly. When he spoke, she could feel the tremors of his deep voice in her own throat. "It was her favorite restaurant. She'd order a few yellowtail and some eel. And she'd ask for her root beer in a sake cup." *She's just a rotting corpse on wings*, Mabel thought.

"Shhh," Wyatt said, reaching around Mabel's knees to turn up the radio. "I want to hear this." As it turned out, two tornadoes had touched down in the night miles away, kicking up whole farms and trailer courts, driving trucks into trees, snapping the necks of horses and cows. "The tiny town sparkles with the dusting of broken glass," said the radio reporter, like some foreign correspondent in a war-torn city, stepping through the wreckage and speaking in near whisper. "The wind left everything in disarray. A man and his son attempt to push their Chevy off the roof of their house. A woman plays her piano in a tree. Some children make a fort of a refrigerator on its back in a schoolyard."

Mabel felt the scratch of chapped lips at her ear. *Everything's ruined*, she heard in the *glug-glug* of a voice underwater. Though Mabel knew her house had not been in the path of the tornado, she began to see things from the shop in the road and the ditches, things she kept locked in a fire-safe box along with the fake suicide note—a necklace of military dog tags her father had once ordered from an ad in a comic book; the press-on nails her mother wore on her honeymoon; the missing glass ruby from an earring Jordan had given Lily.

Mabel felt completely lost, like she'd never find her way home.

She could hardly breathe the damp air in the truck, and she had a headache from the too-strong coffee and from the shrill whistle of the rain getting in through the cracked back window. Mabel pulled at the T-shirt tight at her throat, and she felt Callie's angel wing brush the back of her neck. She felt Callie's soaked strands of hair against her cheek. If the ghost were real, Mabel would've grabbed it by the ankle for them all to see the dead thing Callie had become. *They still wouldn't believe it,* Callie glug-glugged in Mabel's ear, *even if they saw it.*

Callie took Mabel by the scruff of the neck and carried her up so she could look down upon herself crammed into the truck. If they hit a deer and went rolling, not even the jaws of life would be able to pry them all apart. The Roseleafs were too at ease with Mabel's lie and with her presence—the truth would be much too unsettling for them. To tell them the truth now, she thought, would be too absolutely cruel. She'd lie to them and lie to them until she was dead, if it meant saving them another minute of despair.

Roughed around by the bumpy ride, Mabel became more pinned in, one arm behind her back, the other behind Wyatt's, her legs under Jesse's. She couldn't move an inch and had to gasp, practically, for air. Mabel had first developed claustrophobia years before when she'd dared Lily to crawl into the trunk of a junked car on the farm. The girls, each with a BB gun, had been shooting out the car's windows and, with almost all the glass in pieces, they became bored. Lily, of course, accepted the dare. Though the trunk did not close all the way, though Lily got plenty of air and sunlight and had plenty of room in the spacious trunk, Mabel had passed out in the open air and wind of the field.

Wyatt drove into Stitch Farm, past the parking lot, splashing mud and tearing up footpaths. The gates to the lean-to had already been opened, and a crowd had gathered at the back of Mr. Stitch's pickup. When Wyatt hit the brakes, poor dead Callie fell forward, through the windshield, and smack down, face first on the hood of the truck. Seeing the bottoms of her tiny wrinkled feet, pink babyish feet strangely untouched by decay, Mabel pitied Callie and wished she'd been able to make her pretty for the crowd. Mabel could have put a French braid in her thinning hair and rubbed some lipstick into her skin to pinken her cheeks.

"I only wanted some quiet evenings in your house," Mabel said as Wyatt helped her from the truck, out into the rain, her legs still sleepy and numb from the tight ride. "A cocktail and a movie, a haircut on Sunday." Mabel worried that Callie would now haunt her every minute spent in the Roseleaf house, would possibly even drown her in the empty pool as she slept.

"What are you talking about?" Wyatt said, holding Mabel tight by the arms. "You'll spend lots of time in our house. You're part of our life now."

"No," Mabel said, and she leaned in close to Wyatt's ear.

"I'm not part of anything. I lied about having your sister's eye, and you fell for it, that's all. That's all it was. That's all I'm part of." Mabel even stood back to chuckle about it, so he'd think she was sick.

Wyatt dropped his hands from her arms. He just stood there in the rain, his teeth chattering, waiting for her to take it all back. Then, "Shhh," he said, though Mabel had only been whispering. "Hush, now," and he pushed her wet hair back hard from her face. "You're lying. You're just trying to get out of going up to Brandi." He shrugged his shoulders. "You're just telling a little fucking lie."

"I'm not lying," Mabel said. "I mean . . . I mean, I am lying, but . . ." Mabel looked out, hoping to see Callie wuthering above the black umbrellas of the crowd, hoping she'd swoop down to whisper truth in Wyatt's ear.

"Shhh," he said, holding her arms tight again and looking at his brothers and his father waiting at the edge of the crowd. "You just don't want her to touch your eye," he said. Wyatt took Mabel by the elbow. He pushed through the crowd, dragging her to the back of the Stitch pickup, where Brandi sat in her wheelchair. Brandi wore a plastic slicker, see-through over her ratty cashmere suit. Her newly done-up curls were tucked inside a clear hat. Mr. Stitch stood next to her wearing a red and white rain poncho meant for watching college football games. The hood was big enough to cover his entire cowboy hat. Though a few boys held umbrellas above them both, they all got pretty well sopping.

Mr. Stitch took a cameo brooch held up to him by a young

woman, and he pressed it into Brandi's hand. He leaned over, putting his ear to Brandi's mouth. "Mums," Mr. Stitch said that she said. "Mums."

"Oh, dear, yes," the young woman said, taking back the brooch. "Oh, yes. We planted mums next to the grave."

"She must like them," Mr. Stitch said, and the woman nodded and thanked him.

Wyatt shoved Mabel up to the edge of the tailgate, and she saw that Brandi's hand bled from a pricking of the pin of the cameo. "She's the one with the eye," Wyatt told Mr. Stitch, before stepping back. Mabel wondered if there'd been others—the one with the liver, the one with the kidneys. She wondered if she was just the next in a long line of women claiming to have Callie's parts. *Feel her heart beating in my chest*, they may have said, or, stretching out a long leg, *Her marrow's in my bones*, because the Roseleaf boys were so handsome and sad and distant.

Mabel took Brandi's hand and squeezed it, hoping for her to squeeze back, but her grip remained limp. Mabel squeezed harder, but nothing. Brandi only blinked the rain from her lashes. Mabel saw goose pimples across the skin of Brandi's bare legs, and she noticed how long her legs were, how tall she'd be if she stood.

As the rain fell heavier and the wind blew, Brandi's teeth began to rattle. Mr. Stitch put his ear to her lips. "What do you say, darling?" he said, shouting for the benefit of the crowd. "What do you see?"

"She wants you to tell them all the truth," Mabel said, almost convincing herself that the words in her head, the thoughts, belonged to Brandi. She tried to feel some sign of strength in Brandi's hand, some unspoken message in a touch returned. "She wants you to tell them that she doesn't speak to the dead. She doesn't know anything about the dead." There wasn't an ounce of determination in Brandi's face, the face of someone dumb to everyone dead and alive. But Mabel suspected that her own sudden and deep hatred of Mr. Stitch was actually Brandi's. "She wants you to tell them to quit coming to her. Tell them to go home and to stay home and to leave her the fuck alone." Mabel felt a twitch in Brandi's finger then, and she reached up and pulled on Brandi's elbow, intending to take her from her chair, to catch her in her arms and carry her far away to someplace dry and warm. But Brandi was heavy, her useless legs awkward, and Mabel lost her balance, dropping them both into the mud.

Mr. Stitch took a whistle from his pocket, and he blew on it, his face red, the whistle sputtering, and some broad-shouldered young men came running. Three of the men gently lifted Brandi and passed her up to two others next to the wheelchair. Mabel lay on the ground and watched it happen slowly above her—mud rolling with the rain off the plastic slicker, Brandi's unnecessarily orthopedic shoe slipping off her heel, a run sudden in her stocking.

Wyatt was suddenly at Mabel's side, helping her up from the ground. "We gotta get you out of here," he said, "before the mob tears you apart." Mabel slapped Wyatt's hands away and ran toward the open, empty field. She kept running, even after she'd run far away, even after it had stopped raining. A few miles from Stitch Farm, Mabel looked back and saw nothing but cornfields and fields of beans and sorghum. A clumsy locust flew fast into Mabel's shoulder and dropped to the road. It landed on its wings and kicked its legs. *Come back*, it chirped, and Mabel realized it was Callie. *We'll have slumber parties. We'll tell ghost stories.*

Mabel remembered then how tired she was and how hungry, and she promised herself she'd stop seeing Callie, and hearing her, once she'd had some rest and a bite to eat. She kicked the felled locust into the ditch and walked farther, until she came upon a field of sunflowers. The flowers were tall and burned from the sun, the heads bowed and heavy with seed. Mabel picked out the seeds of one and ate them one by one from her palm, sitting in the thin shade of the field.

When Mabel woke up some hours later on the ground beneath the sunflowers, it was dark, and she could hear the cattle of the meat research facility lowing in their pens. A train passed somewhere nearby, and the ground gently shook with every crack of the rail. Mabel got back on the road and found a bottle, which she broke against a post to form a jagged edge. Normally she wasn't afraid of the empty spaces of a country night, but tonight the dark seemed suspect. On an odd night like this one, the thoughts of even the kindliest farmer could turn toward molestation upon coming across a lone girl in the middle of nowhere.

Mabel cut across the empty fields, passing all the old barns that leaned toward the ground just a few strong gusts from collapse. She slapped at the grasshoppers sticking to her legs. When she saw the old shot-up sign for the antique shop, ANTIQUES 2 MI., and the red arrow pointing, Mabel began to run again, though she could hardly lift her feet, she was so tired.

From the end of her driveway, Mabel heard the phone ringing. She thought it might be Lily. *I had a bad feeling*, Lily would say when Mabel answered. But on the phone was a woman offering free dance lessons. "Learn to swing, to tango, to cha-cha-cha; learn hundreds of waltzes, from the Tennessee to the Viennese, learn a country two-step, even a Russian tarantella," all delivered with a genuine flair of enthusiasm. After hanging up on the woman, Mabel worried about not knowing even a single waltz. It was almost as if, in her tired legs, she could feel this absence of knowledge.

Mabel looked across the shop. She could feel the weight of every last little piece of junk. She covered her mouth to keep from breathing in the fog of dust clouding the room. Her clothes caked with dry mud, she sat on the floor and brought her knees in to her chest. Mabel heard the house cracking and popping its joints (*It's just the house settling*, her grandmother had always said), and she felt all the house's age and effort in her own elbows and knees.

On the radio, the reporter had described people setting fire to the feeble remains of their homes after the tornadoes. The people picked through the wreckage for everything sentimental, then let the walls and rafters turn to smoke. Mabel thought about dropping a match on everything around her. How else could she find her rightful place, while this place still stood?

Mabel wondered if the Roseleafs would find it easier to forgive her if she lost everything in a fire. She'd tell them about the original Kewpie that, had its belly not been broken in and the point of its head not chipped off, would've been worth a fortune. And the few broken stained glass pieces, kept in a fishbowl, of a Tiffany window that had once adorned a mausoleum in the famous Woodlawn National Cemetery of New York. When you held one piece up to the light, Mabel would tell them, you could see the red blossom of a tree. Mabel could inventory the loss for the Roseleafs—the lace-up boot of a woman who'd almost taken the *Titanic*, the long curling string snapped from Leadbelly's guitar—so they would understand the near worth of the place. Mabel needed them to worry about her.

Sitting on the floor, Mabel noticed a tiny figure beneath the corner of a rug—the little Swiss girl that Lily had broken from the wheel of a clock when they were little girls. Mabel put the wooden piece in her own mouth, just like Lily had done, rolling it around on her tongue, knocking it against her teeth. This tiny figure would be the one thing she'd keep, Mabel decided. She'd keep it for years, then drop it into Lily's casket should she die first.

Mabel stood and grabbed a red Formica chair and threw it

out the front door, and watched as it bounced a few times down the front walk. She put a brick in front of the screen door to keep it open, then grabbed a box full of matchless shoes and spilled them all out onto the porch. She flung record albums spinning out the window. She grabbed one end of a sofa and pulled it from the house, its legs screeching against the wood floor. Mabel stumbled on the shoes on the porch, but after much struggle she got the sofa out on the lawn.

Enough, Mabel thought, feeling exhausted again. She sat on the sofa and looked up at the moon. Mabel decided she'd give herself a few days to get everything out of the front room. Then she'd begin to turn the place into a respectable shop without clutter or dust. For too long, there'd been too much; if you touched one thing, a whole wall of junk would come tumbling down. She remembered a shop she'd visited in Lincoln, where the proprietor, an old woman smelling of violets, served tea in chipped cups and tricked you with a dish of glass candy. Everything had its own place on a shelf. With thin pieces of string, the woman had tied yellow price tags to everything, and there were no negotiations. Everything was as is.

Mabel smelled smoke and ash and looked up to catch sight of herself tossing something aflame from her bedroom window. It was paper burning, and it spun and floated like a slow Chinese firework toward the ditch of dry grass, where the flame would build and gain force. Though the paper burned, Mabel could read it as it drifted past her vision, could read every bit of the suicide note her mother had written for her father, every old lie and wrong word red and hot.

She curled up on the sofa on the lawn to sleep a minute and dreamed of swimming in the burning house, grabbing at the antiques that floated away and out of reach.

19.

WHEN LILY WOKE, THE FRONT ROOM of her mother's house smelled of burned twigs. A peach sat on the windowsill near the sofa, and beneath it a slip of paper. Lily bit into the fruit, then licked at the juice that ran down her wrist. *Dear Lily,* the note read. *A peach, and there's more in the kitchen closet. I've gone to the vineyard*—and nothing more, not even a "Love, your mother."

As Lily soaked in the tub, she held a sliver of pink soap in her palm, sniffed at its lilac perfume. Earlier, she'd noticed the lipstick on the coffee cup in the kitchen sink and the imprint of her mother's teeth on a triangle of wheat toast. She was determined to learn something significant from these fragments, to bring home to Mabel a useful impression of their mother.

As she unknotted the rats in her hair with her mother's comb, a young pregnant woman stepped into the bathroom.

"Lily," the woman said. Her gauzy white blouse was draped in layers across her wide belly, and she wore pink pants.

"I'm Ana," she said. "Fiona's stepdaughter. Or near stepdaughter. She only lived with my dad for a while. They were never married." With the smooth lilt of Ana's accent, Lily suspected she'd been the one her mother had called the night before, the one to whom she'd spoken Spanish. This Ana had been in the picture with Fiona and the ocean.

"My mother's not here," Lily said, proprietary, stressing the *my*. This possessiveness—it was something stepsisters did to each other, Lily imagined.

"I'm here for *you*," Ana said, taking a chenille robe from a hook on the door. She held the robe open for Lily. Though Ana looked to be Lily's age, she seemed years older, and Lily felt too embarrassed to request privacy. Ana would likely be the type of woman to scoff at modesty, so Lily stood from the tub and put her arms through the sleeves.

"My mother sent you?"

"No," Ana said. She took a tissue from her purse and held it to Lily's chin. Lily spit out the peach pit she'd been distractedly rolling around in her mouth all morning. "Fiona said you were here, and I had a feeling you'd be left alone." Ana sniffed the burned-smelling air. "She's been burning sage," Ana said. "She burns sticks of sage and smokes the place out. To ward off something or other." Ana rolled her eyes.

Lily dressed as Ana hurriedly and fiercely scrubbed at the dishes in the sink. Lily's mother had written of new fiancés over the years but never new daughters. She hoped there were not others; she didn't want to have to imagine Fiona mothering hordes of other people's children.

They drove the short drive to Nogales in Ana's Chevy Nova, a dashboard hula girl swishing wildly with the bumps in the road. Ana played a tape of a girl Lily had never heard of before. "Sugar Pie DeSanto," Ana explained. "It was only the sixties, and already she wasn't taking no shit off anybody." They rocked in their seats to a song called "Do I Make Myself Clear?" and shared a cigarette. "I'm not inhaling deep," Ana said, and she pointed her thumb to her gut. "The boss don't smoke."

Ana tugged at the collar of her blouse, as if she wanted Lily to be sure to notice the bruise. Once, Lily, drunk, fell in the street and broke her glasses—she got a black eye and lived it up, Mabel bringing her shots of Maker's Mark for the pain while she nursed the bruise with a rib eye. Lily wore her clip-on sunshades indoors and out until the bruise faded, all the while enjoying all the quick half glances she got and the behind-the-hand whispers. She'd tell people the truth, like she was telling a lie: *I just fell in the street*, with a mumble, and a crack in her voice. Where did Mabel and I get our sense of drama? Lily wondered. Their mother clearly hoped for her own grief to go entirely unnoticed.

As Lily and Ana stepped onto the crowded sidewalks of Nogales, a small pack of children tugged at their sleeves. They begged them to buy one of the maracas in the trays slung around their necks. Lily accidentally stumbled into them, tipping over a one-armed boy, sending his maracas spinning and rattling into a gutter. Ana quickly righted the boy before he'd even realized he'd fallen, speaking in Spanish and pressing dollar bills into the boy's one palm to stop any fuss. She then linked her arm through Lily's, fanning her with a paper fan patterned with various sumo-wrestling moves. Her eyes closed, Lily lifted her chin to feel the slightly cool push of air against her neck.

"I feel fine," Lily said, though she felt sick from the press of the desert heat. She longed for her own bed and for Mabel's worthless stomach-flu remedies.

Women in braids and housedresses cluttered the sidewalks with souvenirs for sale—ceramic lizards painted in tropical colors, tall bottles of clear vanilla, faceless rag dolls with MEXICO sewn into their skirts. Shopkeeps dragged out piles of blankets that looked scratchy. Terra-cotta suns hung alongside hanging pots spilling out clay fish. The shops sold crescent moons made of frosted glass and chess sets made of rock. Skeleton brides and grooms hung slack jawed from puppet strings.

Lily saw an old movie poster she wanted to buy for Mabel—UN GATO SOBRE EL TEJADO CALIENTE, with an illustration of Elizabeth Taylor in a baby-blue slip sitting on an iron bed. ESTA ES MAGGIE LA GATA. But when she asked Ana, who had firm hold of her arm, to slow down, Ana couldn't hear her weak voice above the racket of the street. Ana only smiled and said, "Just let me know if you want to stop for anything."

Lily touched Ana's stomach without her seeming to notice. She became determined to coax Ana back to

Nebraska with her, where they would all raise the little one together. Lily would be saving Ana, and possibly the child, from abuse, in a way that Lily's mother seemed unable to do. Ana *had* to come with her. There were no other meaningful conclusions.

They walked up to a man who carried a row of counterfeit Gucci handbags on a broomstick at his shoulder. "Medical prescriptions?" the man whispered in Lily's ear, his breath smelling sweetly of clove. "Xanax, Valium?" Ana stepped in to negotiate for a new purse. Mabel would love Nogales, Lily thought—all the bartering, all the cheap goods she could make a fortune off back home in the shop.

Ana, with two handbags on her arm, led Lily to a window in a bright blue wall. She bought them both fish tacos from the walk-up café then led them to a bench in an open space. As they ate the tacos, they watched children practice drums in a schoolyard.

"Are you having a boy or girl, do you think?" Lily said.

"A boy," Ana said. "And don't I know it. The little squirt's been hell on wheels." She gave her stomach an annoyed finger thump.

"You'll be glad to let him out."

"I guess so," Ana said. "But I kind of like him right where he is, truth be known."

"Where'd you get that bruise?" Lily said, feeling a little bold.

"Bruise?" Ana said. She said it like she didn't know what Lily was talking about, but she'd reached right up to the purple spot near her throat. "Oh, this bruise," she said, after a second. "Danny and me, we get to wrestling around. Just horsing around and making out. Just him being cute, and I bruise easily." Ana pressed lightly on the bruise, seeming pleased with it, maybe picturing the romantic rough-and-tumble she described.

It pissed Lily off that Ana, who clearly had some fierce bones in her body, would fall patsy to some guy. "If I was pregnant," Lily said, "I'd protect my baby with my life."

Ana had been leaning in toward Lily, and now she leaned away. "Is that so," Ana muttered, looking off, shutting down. She buttoned her blouse up more, hiding her bruise away.

"Leave the bastard," Lily said, wanting to be the tough stepsister, in town only a minute, who suggested things no one else would. Now Lily wished she'd brought Jordan along, for everyone to envy her her gentle husband. "My sister and me, we have a house, a shop. Come to Nebraska with me."

Ana only shrugged. "Fiona's right about you."

"What do you mean? What is she right about?"

"Nothing," Ana said, keeping it secret. Lily actually relaxed, happy that her mother had formed an opinion of her and had confided it to her closest friend.

"I can give you my address," Lily said. "And you could come anytime. You should do something. Get a gun or something at least."

"Are you crazy?" Ana said. She took out her paper fan again but kept the breeze to herself. Lily leaned over a bit for some of the cooler air. "I'm surprised you'd suggest a gun," Ana said, not looking at Lily. "Your father's suicide and all."

"My mom told you about that?"

Ana shut the fan and dropped it into her lap. She looked at Lily. "She told me things she didn't even tell you."

"What are you talking about?" Lily said.

Ana busied herself with her new purse, concentrating on adjusting the strap. Her hands shook as she fumbled with a tiny buckle. What she said then, she said so softly Lily couldn't hear her. Lily asked Ana to say it again. Ana said, loud enough, but without looking at Lily, "He shot himself in front of her. Your father shot himself right in front of your mother."

"Oh, God," Lily said, losing her breath a second. She'd never had to picture any of it before; no one had ever breathed a word of such violence. In Lily's childish imaginings, the bullet had slipped from the gun down her father's throat like a fatal dose. Lily had never heard who found him or how they'd found him. Now all the parts of the room, long since forgotten, the rust-stained wallpaper, the houseflies thick in summer, a dusty seashell, and a jar of wheat pennies all surrounded her father in his evening chair. How closely had her mother stood, and how closely had she seen? *Come back*, had he said, *or I swear I'll do it*?

"She lied to you," Lily said. "My father would never do that to her."

"She couldn't have been lying to me," Ana said. "Not the way she told it. And Fiona doesn't lie."

"But Fiona always lies," Lily said. "All she does is lie." Lily noticed new things about Ana then, like a patch of broken blood vessels on her neck and a fresh scar at the corner of her eye. The piercing of her ear was torn clear through the lobe.

Ana stood and tossed her taco wrapper into a trash can, then walked toward another street of merchants. Lily still felt dazed from thoughts of her father's sad act of cruelty. She was still back in that room with her father's work boots kicked off by the door, the laces still in knots.

Lily didn't follow Ana. She stood from the bench and slipped into a dark, corner shop silent but for the water running in the fountains for sale. The air in the room was cool and damp, nearly misty. Lily walked past a collection of porcelain sink basins on the floor, the insides painted with flowers and fish and cherubs. After stopping at a wall of tile-framed mirrors, she noticed the dirt in the creases of her face. She took a pack of Kleenex from her purse, licked a tissue, cleaned up a little. Her father, one night, wiped hard at the corn dust, at the red chaff and dirt on her face and neck, enraged at her for playing in the bin. "Children suffocate," he said.

It had been a poker night on somebody's farm, and the grown-ups listened to the old Redd Foxx records the children weren't allowed to hear. Shooed out into the dark for a game of "Ghostie, Ghostie, Come Out Tonight," a boy led the five or so children to the mostly empty corn bin, and he opened the door and removed some of the top panels that kept the corn in. They all stripped and dropped naked into the chest-high pile of shelled kernels. A bird, caught at the top, fluttered its wings against the dark bin walls towering above them. The children, barely lit by a touch of moonlight, walked around like zombies, silent and slow in the thick corn dust. Lily had held her hands close to her chest and burrowed, loving the silkiness of the corn against her skin as it parted and engulfed her.

Lily saw, in the mirror, a girl sitting on the floor of the shop. The girl, her tray of maracas beside her, ate pieces of candied fruit from a paper napkin unfolded in her lap. She offered Lily a piece of sugary mango. As Lily sat on a bench to eat it, she thought of her father that night holding her tight as he scrubbed the chaff away with a dry towel. "I'm not mad," he'd said, very mad, picturing his babies not breathing.

In the corner of the shop, a tall screen painted with red parrots hid a desk. Lily could see a woman's sandaled foot and a curl of adding-machine tape inching down the side of the desk. "Hello?" Lily said, and the woman peeked around.

"Yes?" she said. "Can I help you with something?"

"Where could I find a ride?" Lily asked. "I need to go to Saint Adelaide's," then she added, "to see the nuns," then, "I've left my husband." When the woman still seemed unmoved, Lily lied just a little more. "And I'm pregnant."

The woman then nodded slowly and disappeared again behind the screen. She shouted something in Spanish, her words echoing up a stairwell. She stepped out with her keys. "When my son comes down to watch the shop," the woman said, "I'll drive you up there myself."

"Thank you," Lily said, touched by the woman's gullibility. At Saint Adelaide's, she'd get into the Monte Carlo and vanish from the desert. *She just ran away?* her mother might ask Ana, puzzled by her mysterious daughter. Lily took from her purse the Kleenex with the peach pit from the piece of fruit her mother had left her for breakfast. She'd leave the pit on the dash of her mother's car. Though Lily did feel sympathy for her mother, and what her mother had had to see, nothing had really changed; her mother had still left them in a house full of junk. None of this was very complicated, Lily promised herself.

15.

WHEN MABEL WOKE, STILL ON THE SOFA on the lawn in front of the house, she found that someone had covered her with a thin bathrobe. The robe was patterned with stars and crescent moons and had been food for moths for years as it hung on a coat hook. Mabel's eye caught on a bicycle dropped near the porch, a wheel slowly spinning to a stop. She noticed a crumb of something on the porch step.

Of a muffin, Mabel realized, picking up the crumb and putting it in her mouth. With a blueberry. Mabel's stomach rumbled, and her shoulders and back ached from the night on the sofa, but she felt wonderful, accomplished, seeing the scattered shoes and the records on the grass. Soon the house would be empty of its boxes of broken dishes and the rolled carpets in the rafters. She would toss out the tobacco tins full of snapshots of long-dead strangers and the basket of glass percolator tops collected off old coffee pots. As Mabel walked back into her house, she closed her eyes and subtracted everything from the image in her mind. She slowly and carefully felt her way down the path in the junk, avoiding the corners of shelves and the legs of tables. The house would be a place of potential, her life one of promise.

Mabel followed a scent of coffee and red pepper, and she opened her eyes. Atop the kitchen table were more crumbs of muffin and part of a breakfast burrito still warm from the Texaco microwave. Mabel sat down to drink the coffee dregs from the Styrofoam cup and to eat the last bites of the food. Not until she ate all there was did she wonder who had been in her house.

Looking around the room, she noticed a paper sack she didn't recognize on the floor next to the stairs; inside was the metal lettering pried from the backs and sides of deluxe cars—CADILLAC in gold-plated cursive, and MERCEDES and PORSCHE. She saw then, on the stairs, a trail of clothes—jeans, T-shirt, boxer shorts with heart shapes. When she got to the fringed moccasins, she knew Jordan was back. He was always buying hand-beaded moccasins; he liked to go out to the reservation to play the illegal slots and to get the government-issue peanut butter for cheap. Mabel picked up his clothes from the steps, along with a bent-up Polaroid photo of Lily and Jordan with a black bottle of Cava beneath a crepe-paper bell. A quickie wedding along the way, and me left uninvited. *How not surprising,* Mabel thought, surprised. Strangers for witnesses and canned wedding hymns. The bridal bouquet tossed into a pack of rented well-wishers. But Mabel was too glad to have Lily and Jordan back to be at all aloof or punishing. "You're home," she said, pressing her cheek against the closed bathroom door. "You're home."

"Come in," Jordan shouted out, "but don't come near me. I've got lice."

Jordan sat naked in the empty tub, his hair standing on end with a thick shampoo. He'd covered his privates with a *Penthouse* magazine. "I'd give you a little kiss," he said, "but I'm infested. I've got to sit dripping with this shampoo for ten minutes. I'm thinking of going to the filling station next to shower in gasoline. Anything to kill the damn parasites." He spoke quickly and his tongue sounded like it was too heavy to lift around his words. Mabel wondered if he was hopped up on something. "I hope it's all right that I came here," he said. "I stole a bike from in front of the bus station. My dad's going to be pissed off at me for leaving town, even though he did fire me. So I'm trying to avoid him. Though I could use him to float me a loan. Tell you what . . . if he gives me some money, I'll take us all out for steaks . . . my treat. I know you love steak."

"Where's Lily?" Mabel said, holding out the Polaroid, to let him know that she knew.

"I don't care," he said, looking away. "Lily's dead to me." Then he said, "Not really. It's just that she left me behind, in the middle of the night, without a word of good-bye." Then he added, "In Vegas, on our honeymoon," he said, his eyes wide with romantic misery. Jordan held up his hand. "You don't want to hold me," he said. "You don't want this lice."

But Mabel had had no intention of going to him—she was struck cold with worry for Lily. It was easier when she could imagine Lily and Jordan gone off together. Mabel thought of the things of Lily's she'd kept over the years: a baby tooth, an old barrette with strands of Lily's hair caught in its clip. When she was little, Mabel had heard such things were useful to investigators looking for lost children. If Lily had ever turned up missing, Mabel could have offered the police a chewed-on pencil and a photocopy of the palm of Lily's hand.

"Did you see the stuff I brought you back from Vegas?" Jordan said, cheering slightly. "The lettering in the paper sack? I collected that stuff myself. I figured you could sell it in the shop. The kids buy that stuff and wear it as jewelry."

Mabel noticed Jordan's skin was splotchy pink and red. She picked up an empty bottle of shampoo from the floor—SAV-MOR LICE KIT. "You're only supposed to use a little bit," she said, reading the directions.

"I know," he said, with a sigh. "I've probably OD'd on the stuff. But I could still fucking feel them crawling on me, after two whole treatments." He held up his hands and bent and unbent his fingers, wiggling them, making them buggy. "They're all over my fucking body. I just know I got 'em from sitting next to this one filthy friggin' Boy Scout on the bus."

"I'm a little worried," Mabel said. "You shouldn't have used so much of this stuff. It's toxic." Must his every action tend toward the suicidal? Even the taking of his medicine? How could she care so much about someone so precariously perched in the world? "You're even talking funny," she said.

"Oh," and Jordan's shoulders shook as he looked down with a silent laugh. "Oh, that." He looked back up at her and opened his mouth wide. Mabel resisted the urge to reach out and touch the piercing, the tiny silver ball near the tip of his tongue. "When I was sitting in the hotel lobby, waiting for Lily to come back, I read a *Cosmopolitan* magazine that somebody had left laying there on a table. There was this article that recommended getting something pierced as a cure for heartbreak." He lowered the magazine a bit so she could see the silver hoop piercing his navel, an outie that Mabel had always thought so adorable, so childlike. Then he turned his head around so she could see his left earlobe stuck through with a gold stud and the ring around the top of his ear. "If I knew you a little better," he said, winking, nodding at the magazine at his crotch, "I'd let you see the one down below." Then he laughed and said, "I'm just kidding. I'm not so heartbroken as to mutilate that."

He'd come back to Mabel and, no surprise, Lily had literally filled him full of holes first. "You shouldn't have done it to your belly button," Mabel said. "It was cuter before." She turned toward the door and said, "You better wash this stuff off."

"You could stay a minute," Jordan said, smiling and biting his lip, trying to seem cute and boyish. "Help me comb out my nits." Then he kind of laughed, so she'd know he was just joking about the combing.

If all this had happened on some other day, maybe only days before, Mabel might have taken her sister's husband naked and scrubbed to her bed and run her tongue over his, over all the metal pieces in his body, and over the scar on his wrist. She would have let him shut his eyes tight, let him keep his hands to himself, and would have let him think of whomever he wanted to think of.

Mabel did still long to kiss him but only to know what his new tongue felt like. She'd kiss him once, she thought, and keep the kiss as a souvenir. "Can I try it?" she said, tapping her finger at her own tongue, kneeling beside the tub. Jordan smiled and opened his mouth on hers. *A soft tongue breaks the bone*, Mabel remembered her mother, in her religious phase, quoting whenever Mabel and Lily screamed in argument. *A soft tongue*, she thought, kissing Jordan, jimmying the cold metal bump, and she thought of the next line in Proverbs, a question she'd found when looking up her mother's strange admonitions in her Girl's First Bible. *Have you found honey*? was the question. Though the Proverb had gone on to speak of excess and vomit, Mabel had always loved the sound of it: *Have you found honey?* God asks in his gentle interest.

Mabel leaned back and wiped her lips with the back of her hand, feeling a sharp bite of headache from the chemical shampoo. She wouldn't be his agonizing guilt, his little cruelty. He'd have to find some other way to hurt Lily.

Mabel said to Jordan, "Some people shave their heads to get rid of lice."

Jordan looked toward the ceiling, squinting, probably seeing himself with all his hair gone and looking tough and angry. "Would you shave my head for me, Mabel?" When she nodded, he pulled the plastic curtain closed and turned on the shower to rinse off the shampoo.

Mabel got the blue case from under the sink and took out the electric clippers. She was anxious to see the true shape of Jordan's head, and she hoped the transformation was shocking. When Jordan finished rinsing off, he reached from around the curtain to grab a towel to wrap around his waist, and he sat on the edge of the tub, his back to Mabel. "There's a whole industry of porno about shaving," Jordan said, chuckling. Mabel didn't think she was a fetishist, but she did like the ritual of this afternoon haircut, the almost sacred act of specific order—the steam in the room and the buzzing of the clippers, the hair falling away in wet curls, the cold smell of the menthol burning her nose. After cutting the hair down to the stubs with the electric scissors, she followed the curve of Jordan's skull with her daisy-wheel leg shaver, and she fully understood the meaning of the Roseleafs' monthly haircuts and foreign movies. It was like making your own religion, building your own church in your own rooms.

When she finished, Jordan was smiling even before he looked in the mirror. Mabel had been startled when he'd turned around, and she looked forward to the getting used to it—that slow process of studying someone until they were newly familiar. Jordan touched his head only hesitantly, like he was afraid to feel the shape of the bone. "I think I like it," he said. "I think it makes me look a little crazy." His smile fell then, and he looked sad again.

Mabel slipped from the bathroom without Jordan even

noticing—he was so intent on his reflection. Mabel went to Lily's room and lay back on the bed, and she thought of her father, not a religious man, reading to her and Lily, not from the Bible, but from a slim book called *The Blue Book of Fairy Tales*. Mabel would lean against his arm to see the illustrations of characters who looked wan and wanting even after their lives were bettered.

Mabel thought of Rose-Red and Snow-White often in the forest alone gathering red berries. *No mishap ever overtook them*, her father read. The first day Lily was gone, Mabel had cleaned and straightened Lily's bedroom, and now Mabel decided to put it back the way it was. When Lily came back, she'd be comfortable, knowing her room was left untouched. Mabel took the clothes she'd washed and hung and she tossed them back on the floor. She rehung a sheer nightie that had been left hanging in the window at the end of the curtain rod. She unmade the bed, and she knocked over the stack of magazines next to the nightstand. She moved around the perfume bottles atop the vanity, taking out the stoppers, knocking a few over. She picked up the newspaper clipping she'd left on Lily's pillow, and she crumpled it up and shoved it in her pocket. A small plane had gone down off the coast of Virginia, the clipping reported. A mother of one of the crash victims said that her daughter had been booked for an earlier flight, but had been late. "She's always running late," the mother was quoted as saying.

16.

LILY DROVE MORE THAN TWENTY-FOUR hours nearly nonstop, existing mostly on liters of Jolt cola. The few minutes she slept sitting up at a rest stop had been long enough to dream of her father and her mother in a dry desert garden. Her mother tore the husk from a tomatillo and held the little green apple-like thing to her father's teeth black with gun powder. Her father dipped her mother in a tango, the blood keeping his hair matted atop his half a head, and he whispered *My little piece-of-shit cunt* in her ear, and she giggled at the sweet nothing.

On the road, Lily played the radio, hooking onto a station and staying with it until she could only hear a few words here and there spoken or sung amid the static. As each station dissolved, she hesitantly moved on to another, when there was another, and got to know the other towns somewhere up ahead or around. She learned the jingles of businesses she would never patronize and the names of the streets on which they could be found, and she'd devise little lives for herself—the three-dollar breakfast steak at Kitty's Knife and Fork before 6, then off to her free guava juice with every kiwi-acid facial at the Electric Beach Tan & Spa, then shopping for dresses and deep-discount electronics at the Sun on the Lake Mall. She could follow it all with two-dollar dirty-martini-doubles at Flim's, where she would mention this ad and get a free cigar.

LILY STOPPED at the Motel Modern, only a few hours from home, and stayed for two days. She imagined herself an elegant ruin, a newly divorced woman going by her maiden name and staying at the motel for as long as she could afford. FORWARD ALL MY MAIL TO: LILY ROLLOW, C/O THE MODERN. Cocktails drunk alone at a little table in a safari-theme lounge. Dresses pressed by housekeeping and left hung on the doorknob.

Lily went into town and bought white pajamas and a portable typewriter at a swap meet. She wanted to write her mother a letter; she had no idea what she'd say, but she'd say it in the efficient alphabet of a machine, making her words appear carefully thought out. But when she typed out a test line, *Now is the time for all good men to come to the aid of their country*, the letters floated and fell from the line, looking like a clown act.

Lily stayed in her pajamas all day. She'd close up the curtains tight to block out all sun, and drape her scarf over the tiny lampshade to cast the walls with a pink glow. Lily practiced her palmistry for Omaha. She could spend her weekends in the Old Market, she figured, reading palms and tarot for cheap on the sidewalks in front of the galleries and cafés and antique shops open late. She didn't know much about the technical aspects of palm reading, but she didn't think she really needed to be very good to work the Market—for years a caricaturist had attracted long lines of people who would pose, laughing, anticipating, then step away not recognizing anything about themselves in the scrawls on the page. A carriage driver made a fortune in tips trotting lovers down the rough brick street, around corners of urban decay, the smokelike steam from the stacks of the Campbell's soup factory obscuring the sky. Lily could make a nice living off the sorority girls alone.

Lily stood in front of her room waiting for Irene, the motel owner's flirty teenage daughter who had checked her in. The sky was overcast, and Lily's skin was bubbly neon in the sign's light. A few tiny drops of rain sprinkled against her bare legs and arms and felt like they were touching her from the inside, felt like the needling of limbs fallen asleep.

Irene had claimed to belong to a group of high school lesbians who nightly drank mock menstrual blood (bloody mary mix and sweetened condensed milk) in honor of their saint, Brandon Teena. Brandon, a young woman who'd lived as a boyish, soft-spoken man, had been raped, and later murdered, in a small southeast Nebraska town some years before.

"I'd cut off my penis, if I had one," Irene had growled at the boys flocking at her side the other afternoon, wearing Doc Martens and cut-off Levi's and just a pink lacy bra.

Irene stepped from the back screen door of the motel office, holding a tray with two drinks. "Pink ladies," Irene said. At the top of the plastic swizzle sticks were silhouettes like those on trucker's mud flaps, of busty women in recline. Irene's only cosmetic was the polish chipping from her nails. As she held out the palm of her hand to be read, Lily asked the color of her polish. "Numb," Irene called the freon blue.

Lily tried to see what she could in Irene's palm. Despite having carefully skimmed the book on palmistry, Lily had trouble discerning a fork from a prong, a cutting off from a termination, the girdle of Venus from the mount of the moon. Even with a map of the hand unfolded atop the bed, Lily couldn't remember what anything meant. She measured the lines of Irene's hand with a piece of thread, then thumbed anxiously through her palmistry book.

Lily had wanted to predict something of interest, to reward Irene for her patience, even something sad like childlessness or death in another country. But all she could find in her hand was the possibility of jaundice for one month and maybe disease of the spleen late in life.

Irene took Lily's hand in her own then and ran her finger along the lines of Lily's palm. Irene *hmmm*ed with mock consideration. "Just as I thought. You've got no fucking future in palm reading," she said. Irene turned Lily's hand over and touched at the opaque sphere of the ring Lily still wore.

"What else did you do out west," Irene said, "besides leave your husband?"

"I found my mother," Lily said, though her mother probably hadn't been lost for years. Her mother may have had a few madwoman months wandering the desert, picking imagined pieces of her husband's brain from her hair, but that was all before Ana and the nuns and the years of widowhood like a constant girls' night out.

Lily lay back in the bed feeling—what was the word?—*sanguine*, the word of a lady in a hotel. *The Hotel San Guine*. Sanguinity was something someone like Irene would never know, Lily told herself. Even perfection would not be good enough for Irene; perfect was too close to not quite good enough. Things, for Irene, would have to be better than perfect, *pluperfect?* Words Lily didn't even know rushed into her head to attach themselves to meaning. Lily held her own hand before her face—her inability to decipher anything from the thicket of lines in her own palms, the lines like spilled pick-up sticks, relieved her. Her character, her future, was thankfully etched nowhere in her skin.

17.

BY THE END OF THE AFTERNOON, MABEL and Jordan had emptied much of the shop onto the lawn. Mabel dropped into the Rayette Falcon, a chair of sparkly red vinyl with a clear, cone-shaped hair drier sprouting up from the back of it. She'd found it one day in the alley behind a hair salon. RAYETTE FALCON was written in silver across the cone.

The few people who drove past drove slow, rubbernecking at the sea of junk and THIS JUNK SHOP FOR SALE still in red across the front of the house. These people might wonder what was to become of her. They might speculate about her ambitions. What would they make of it all? Mabel wondered, daydreaming.

Jordan sat cross-legged at Mabel's feet to practice his nail polishing on her toes, anticipating his father hiring him back as manicurist at the barbershop. Despite his break up with

Lily, he seemed to want to make a life for her. Mabel had suggested a proper wedding in the house now that everything had been moved out, and Jordan had just shrugged but had sat on the porch as he'd eaten his lunch studying 1960s and '70s bridal magazines he'd found in a box.

Jordan had wanted to paint Mabel's fingernails, but Mabel didn't feel like having her hands held. She sat in the Rayette Falcon holding a ship in a bottle, uncorked, and she ran her finger through the bottle's dust. A spider had found its way inside and, like a black sea monster, crawled over the mast.

"You could sell all this shit on eBay," Jordan said. "Those Internet junkies will put a price on anything."

Mabel reached into her pocket to feel the little wooden girl from the Swiss clock. She held the girl like a tiny Buddha between her fingers, rubbing it with her thumb, working the luck and the wisdom from it. She wished she'd kept the plastic panther for Lily and had not dropped it down the drain of the Roseleaf pool. When Lily returned, Mabel could show her the front room, empty but for a china cup or a china saucer. Inside the cup could be the Swiss girl lying next to the panther. Tiny things, but Lily would certainly remember them. She would more than remember them. There was no reason to believe that anything so small, anything so long lost so deeply in childhood, could ever resurface. Lily would never, ever expect it.

MABEL TOOK the bicycle from near the front porch and rode the miles toward the Roseleaf Ranch; once there, she would toss the bike in the back of the Jimmy still parked near the pool. She just wanted to sneak back to retrieve Lily's plastic panther from where it stuck in the pool drain, but she wasn't at all afraid of being seen. She welcomed any kind of response from Wyatt, should she see him—disgust, weeping, threats of violence even. She was willing to offer hours of lengthy explanation and begging for forgiveness.

Darkness fell by the time she reached the house, and she rode up next to the Jimmy. She stepped onto the hood to climb up and over the wall and walked to the edge of the pool. The deep end still held rain from the day before, the water brown with muck and dead leaves. The only lights lit in the house were upstairs.

Mabel rolled up the bottoms of her jeans, but when she stepped in, the dirty water reached above the cuffs. She walked lightly, careful to avoid any broken glass or sharp twigs. The shattering reflection of the full, white moon made the water look clear, and she crouched down to lower her head and her tongue to take a drink from the sea of tranquility. Mabel would not have been surprised to see Callie Roseleaf only fractions of inches tall and clinging to the skeleton of a leaf skimming the water.

You had to be in a certain state to receive a ghost, Mabel supposed when she could see nothing unusual in the pool. She lowered her face even further, holding her breath and closing her eyes, feeling the water gently washing her skin with silt and something that felt like ash. Mabel covered her mouth and her nose with her hand and lowered her head to let the water wash in and out her ears. She could only hear her breath moving nowhere.

Mabel kept her head in the water, kept her face covered, and listened to the movement of the nearly still pool. She thought no more of Lily and the panther or even of Callie. She thought of Callie's mother, the mother of those boys, who was too weak to repair anything. Like Mabel's own mother, Mrs. Roseleaf couldn't bear to live in a world where things could go on, could mend, following such great loss. She wanted the pain to stay devastating, that was all. Mrs. Roseleaf loved her boys and her husband. But it wouldn't have been right to let everything fall back into some kind of order. She had to get away as far as she could, to keep everything from being the same again. It was a maternal impulse. Of course it was. A deep desire to keep your dead as a constant ache in your heart, and not just a memory or a pain somewhat eased. It had to always be that thing that ruined your life.

Mabel slowly lifted her head from the water and saw down the hill a bit, to the old playhouse all lit up. Then she noticed Wyatt lying back on the battered patio lounge chair enjoying a beer and a tomato. He took a big bite from the tomato, as if eating an apple. The tomato's juice dribbled down his wrist and his arm.

Mabel and Wyatt met each other at the edge of the pool, and Wyatt pushed back a string of dirty, wet hair from Mabel's cheek. Mabel felt about to cry. She couldn't bring herself to face Wyatt with some lame apology; she should leap from the pool and run away to spend a few days writing a long ad for the classifieds—everything right to say for only nickels a word.

Wyatt offered her a bite from his tomato. "A hothouse red," he said, when she refused. "I've decided to start eating better," he said, then dropped the remains of the tomato into the pool. He took the cigarette from behind his ear and put the butt to the pout of his lip, posing squinty eyed and cocky in the silver light of the moon.

Mabel remembered a photo booth at the Ben Franklin on the town square; a few months after her mother ran away, their grandmother took Mabel and Lily to the variety store and bought them new dresses, dressed them up in the dressing room, then shoved the girls, price tags still dangling, into the booth. "Sit nice," she'd insisted. Then at the post office, she put the black and white photo strip in an envelope, and she made Mabel address it and write a note begging her mother to come back. A few weeks later, Mabel collected the mail and found the envelope returned to sender, her mother having moved once again, the red-stamp hand pointing an accusing finger at Mabel's rural address. But Mabel had liked getting a letter from herself: *We miss you so much*, Mabel had read over and over, and she'd used the photo strip as a bookmark to mark off the days in her diary.

Wyatt took Mabel's hand and led her to the ladder at the side of the pool, where he helped her step out. "No more *huevos rancheros* for me," he said. "No more Tabasco and eggs. I want my organs to be healthy enough to pass on to somebody else when I'm dead, I guess." Mabel wasn't looking at his face, but she could hear the wink in his voice. He handed her the cigarette, and they leaned back against the wall. She held her lips at the filter of his cigarette, not to smoke, but to feel it still wet from his puffing at it.

She returned the cigarette to him, running her fingers against his. "You look tired," Mabel said. He looked roughed up and out of sorts. He wore a fancy Western shirt with pearl snaps and yellow roses hand-painted at the shoulders, but the sleeves had been cut off, and he wore it untucked. He was unshaven, his hair unwashed, his red eyes rubbed sore.

"Jesse kept us up all night again," he said. "There's this waitress at Closed Mondays who had those . . . you know, those Norplants put in her arm as part of her parole." He rubbed his upper arm where the contraceptive would have been implanted. "But they had to take them out because they were making her dizzy all the time. The drug company settled a class-action suit with Norplant users, and she got a check for a couple thousand dollars. When we got back from Stitch Farm, she was waiting here for us, waiting to invite Jesse to move to Portland, Oregon, with her. Fastest growing city in the country, she says. I didn't say a word. Not a word. We just all got drunk on Asti, and I passed out in the tub. I didn't say a word, not even when Jesse told me they were going to stop off in Ogallala to snatch the waitress's boy from his foster folks. Not a word. Not a word from me. Jesse's just got to destroy himself and be fucking done with it already. I can't baby-sit the no-dick little fucker no more."

Mabel glanced over at the house, and the bright light of

an upstairs room gave her spots in her eyes. She wondered if Callie's ghost had returned, transmogrified into the clear lightning bolt that floated at the corners of her vision. "What kind of a person comes up with a lie like the lie I told?" Mabel said, partly under her breath, her voice scratchy. She honestly thought he might have some kind of idea. "Why would anyone lie about something like that? Who would do it?"

"I don't know," Wyatt said. He held her hand and leaned his head against hers. Mabel closed her eyes to see the picture they'd make—a sad pair, lost in monochrome.

"There's this place I know," Wyatt said, "where I go to pray. I mean, I don't really pray to anyone in particular, I just . . . maybe pray is the wrong word."

"I'd love to go," Mabel said. Just then she would have given herself over to any kind of religious indoctrination Wyatt offered up: a cupful of blood, a biscuit of flesh, a baptism in muddy waters, his hand holding her head deep, deep under for salvation.

WYATT DROVE the Jimmy so that Mabel could stick her legs out the window to dry them off some. He took her down an old highway that had once been popular with motorists passing through the state on their way to vacation spots, once a string of roadhouses and drive-up diners. A row of wigwam-shaped motel rooms sat covered in graffiti, their triangular windows broken out and boarded up. A two-story–tall covered wagon, once a filling station and souvenir stand, still stood, one of its giant wheels having fallen off to crush an abandoned Chevy. There used to be a tiny carnival somewhere. Mabel had already been down this highway, scavenging, but had only come back with the pink hoof of a carousel horse.

Wyatt pulled into the lot where the drive-in movie screen still towered above rows of speaker posts. The headlights shone on the rusted, splintered playground equipment lining the bottom of the screen. Someone had spray-painted JESUS SAVES on the screen, and beneath that someone else had painted GREEN STAMPS.

"This is the place," Wyatt said, parking. "But it's dumb, I know."

"It's not dumb," Mabel said, pulling her legs in to hold them against her chest.

"I'd like to make it into something again," he said. "We used to come here when I was a kid. Back before Cody was even born. Callie was just a little thing. She'd sit up front with Mom and Dad, and me and Jesse would sit in the back sharing the popcorn. I loved having my family all together in one place like that, all of us in the car, just to watch some stupid cheap-ass movie. The popcorn tasted dirty, and the soda pop was all watered down, and the speaker popped and was so scratchy you could hardly hear anything right. But any given minute of my life, any given minute, I'd rather be back there. Within inches of my whole family, everyone perfectly content with every worthless thing. I could reach up and fuck with my mom's hair-clip thing, and she'd get pissed. And I could reach over and tickle Callie's neck. Jesse would fall asleep on my arm, and I'd let him, even though he had a big fat heavy head and was a little asshole to me most of the time. During scary movies, Mom would make us cover our eyes, and I'd really do it, you know? I'd cover my eyes and not watch, because she really wanted us not to, and I'd try to imagine what all that sound went with. I'd sit there with my eyes covered, picturing screaming women all bloody and cut and men full of knives and blood in their mouths. Throats cut, arms cut off. But I guess I'll never feel so safe as that again."

Wyatt was leaning toward Mabel, his one hand on the seat between them, open. Mabel touched at the blue vein of his wrist. She wanted so much to kiss him. But he would never be able to even look her in the eye without seeing her complete dishonesty, without seeing much too much going on. She hoped for him to find someone normal to love. He should have someone with some complications but simple complications, easy ones. He should just meet someone, someone kind, and just know right away. Someone good for him.

"Even if I couldn't get it going as a drive-in again," Wyatt said, looking down at their hands touching, "I'd like to do something with it. Even if I just set up a projector over there and showed the foreign movies I used to watch with my dad on Sundays on TV. *Mississippi Mermaid* and 8½, maybe on just a little corner of the screen."

Mabel leaned her head over more, her cheek nearly touching Wyatt's shoulder, and she imagined Wyatt showing his foreign movies while she sold movie memorabilia in the old stucco concession stand. She imagined herself owning little things of interest, like the glasses Burt Lancaster wore in *Sweet Smell of Success* or Shelley Winters's cigarette holder in *Lolita*.

"We might do something about the pool," Wyatt said, out of the blue. "I don't know what. I don't know what people do. Do they fill it with cement? With dirt? Or do they just keep it, and use it, like nothing ever happened? We'll just do what other people do." He closed his hand softly over Mabel's fingers. "Why were you in the pool again tonight?"

"I was looking for something," Mabel said. "Something I dropped the last time."

"What?"

"Just a toy. A plastic little figure, an animal. A panther."

Wyatt didn't say anything for a minute, then reached over to touch at her ear, and his fingers tickled her neck, and she pulled away. He continued to tickle her skin, though, smiling. "You've got something," he said. "Hold still—you've got something there. Just let me get it," and he then held before her face the plastic panther. He grinned wide and chuckled. "Voilà," he said. "A little trick."

Mabel had gone looking for it, but she hadn't wanted to see it ever again, she realized. It should have been lost to them all years ago, buried deep in her father's grave. Mrs. Cecil deserved to be long haunted by it, for taking it from their father's coffin after Lily placed it there at his side. Mabel hoped Mrs. Cecil never slept peacefully again, not a wink, from worry of what thieves would pluck from her own coffin.

Her pretty rings, her cameos and pins, her yellowed love letters, her pressed flowers, any piece of sentiment saved and saved and saved.

"I'm sorry, Mabel," he said. "I'm sorry, sweetie. I didn't mean to upset you. I had thought it was maybe Callie's or Cody's, from when they were kids. I saw it floating in the muck tonight and picked it out of the pool. Here . . . here, have it back, Mabel. I want you to take it back."

"I don't want it," Mabel said, wiping at her tears with the backs of both her hands. "I don't know why I'm crying. It's just that I don't know what the fuck to do with myself. Half the time. You know? I just, you know, I just wander around, I drive around, and now, do you know what I did? I dragged everything out of my house, and dragged it onto the front lawn, and, you know, *now what?* And, okay, so I do something else for a while, I do something else, but you know, there's this sense that . . . fuck, Wyatt," and Mabel leaned closer to Wyatt to whisper, not wanting, really, to say it at all. "There's this sense that the worst hasn't happened yet. But of course it has. It all has to be in the past, doesn't it? The worst? We've had our share, Lily and me. But I don't think it is all in the past. In my heart, I feel there could be something worse. What the fuck am I supposed to do with that? Do other people worry like that?"

Wyatt kissed Mabel on the cheek, then kissed her lips. He held his fingers gently at her chin. Mabel held his other hand, and he squeezed back, almost too hard. They kissed for several minutes there in the Jimmy, and Mabel thought about nothing but where he might touch her next. She wanted to fall in love with him, and she was certain it would happen soon. Someday soon he would tell her things, and she would believe them easily.

18.

AS LILY DROVE HOME, SHE WATCHED a few small birds flying low and stirred into strange patterns by the wind. There were some ancients, Lily had read, who could read the patterns of birds in flight, like reading the settling of tea leaves.

Lily had a vision of the lights of Vegas sprinkling through a threadbare curtain, a name tag still pinned to a sequined bikini top on the floor (HI MY NAME IS *NUEVA*), Jordan wearing only a yellowed, ruffled tuxedo shirt unbuttoned, and opening an envelope of international coffee. Lily's visions were improving, becoming much more vivid.

On the seat next to Lily, a pre-divorce kit bought at a bookstore lay spread out, its forms rustling in the wind from the open window.

But Lily considered just driving on, taking a false name and becoming a missing person. Even if she couldn't make a go of it as a palm reader, she thought, there were other good jobs to be had in a place like Omaha. She could learn some standards and sing lounge somewhere, or she could peddle secondhand comic books in a head shop. There were even some theater troupes that paid their actors. All through high school, Lily had been allowed only to play mothers and grandmothers because she was a little heavy and wore thick glasses. Just thinking of the old high school drama department wigs, so worn they had holes and bald patches, made Lily's head itch.

As she pictured herself shoehorned into her downtown ten-by-twelve rented by the week—drawers that pulled out of the wall, a sofa that converted, blouses hanging from the shower-curtain rod—the antique shop, painted with red letters, swam into view all ripply behind waves of heat. THIS JUNK SHOP FOR SALE, she read, turning onto the country road. Another fit of Mabel's, Lily thought, not at all believing the words on the house.

Lily would act like she hadn't even noticed. She wouldn't entertain a single scolding from Mabel, and she'd pay no heed to Mabel's pouts. She was a grown-up in a rush. A few words about their dear mother and her cute bungalow and her work with the nuns, about the exotic chaos of the streets of Mexico, then an I must be off. Forward all my mail . . .

But when Lily pulled into the drive, she noticed everything gone from the porch, even the swing, and the Coke machine that *ca-chunked* when you pulled out a ten-ounce bottle. Those things weren't supposed to be sold; her grandmother had promised Lily the Coke machine way back when she was a little girl, and the porch swing was for summer nights.

Lily sat in the car a minute to regain her composure. Her last cigarette had nearly torn in half at the bottom of her purse, but Lily lit it anyway, and it sat bent and barely smoking at her lips. *That fucking bitch better not have touched one goddamn thing in my bedroom,* Lily thought, then heard the *tsk-tsk*ing of her mother, and she saw the nuns, a whole murder of them, dressed as they hadn't been, in long black robes with rosaries dangling clear down to their knees.

Lily stormed up the walk. When she opened the front screen door, she saw the room empty but for a salon chair and a bald man painting over the wallpaper. Someone else was living in her house, and she didn't know what to do. She closed the door, then knocked on it, and the so-strange feel of her own screen door rattling under her fist started her to crying. The bald man kept on painting, his back to her. He wore a large pair of radio headphones clamped at his ears, and he swayed a bit to the music he heard.

Lily ran back to the car, sick of crying in front of strangers. She started the car, but Omaha suddenly seemed like a rancid town, the Old Market a place where a person could be left for dead. She could smell the smoke of clove cigarettes and the pepper of patchouli and could hear herself being raped at midnight by a unisex punk with a blue Mohawk twenty years too late. No, Lily wanted to be safe again in her own upstairs room, stripped down to her undies, listening to the Sugar Pie DeSanto tape she'd stolen from Ana's car and drinking Canadian whiskey from a clay goblet Jordan had crafted for her in a pottery class.

When Lily glanced up to her bedroom, she saw her little pink nightie, hand wash only, that she'd hung in the window to dry days before. It caught a breeze and did a short cootchie dance for her. With this evidence of herself still in the house, Lily got out of the car to investigate. She went to a side window to look closer at the bald man painting. He wore no shirt with his bib overalls that didn't fit, the legs at "expecting a flood?" length. When she realized that the man was Jordan, she was filled with worry and confusion—the house had been sold and emptied, and Jordan was full of cancer and chemo. But he looked too healthy; he'd put on some weight in his cheeks, and some pink, and the stringy muscles of his arms twitched with his brush strokes. The buttons at the side of his overalls were undone, flashing a bit of fleshy, naked hip.

But the back of his head seemed just skin and bones, the flesh too close to the skull for Lily's comfort.

Lily pressed her forehead against a pane of glass gone foggy with age, the glass frosty like panes of sugar. Maybe they could take lessons with a priest, Lily thought. She'd heard of earnest newlywed Catholics studying manuals on marriage preparation and getting quizzed in a church office. Lily and Jordan needed such a ritual with an ancient celibate in a room of smoky light and leather-bound books, of hot tea and honey poured in a cup, the cup set in a saucer, the saucer set on the end of a massive desk of dark wood.

Deep in the room of the priest, Lily felt something hit her head, then saw something land near her foot. It was a piece of toast, and she looked up to see Mabel tossing the bread down at her from the roof above the side porch. Mabel sat there with her breakfast outside her bedroom window. "Did you see the salon chair?" Mabel said. "The Rayette Falcon? It's got an ashtray built right into the arm of it."

Mabel tossed another piece of bread at Lily. Lily picked up the crumb and ate it though she'd filled up on the Moons Over My Hammy special at Denny's. Mabel was pretty in a chenille robe, even with the every which way of her hair. She had the segments of an orange atop a paper napkin open on her lap, and at her side was an actual butterfly in a bamboo-looking cage. The butterfly opened and closed its wings slowly and contentedly, with the rhythm of sleeping breath.

Mabel lifted the cage by its short chain, startling the butterfly to thrash its wings against the bars. "I'm starting a new business," Mabel said. "People don't like to toss rice at weddings anymore because the birds eat it, then it blows up in their stomachs. So some brides pay big bucks to have the guests open cages of butterflies on the church steps." Mabel touched at the cage. She shushed at the insect. "I've been feeding her milkweed from the ditch," Mabel said. "I've only been able to find this one, though." Lily had heard about area crops of genetically altered corn that was believed to kill caterpillars with its pollen, threatening the monarch population, but she didn't have the heart to tell Mabel about it. "I've got to make money somehow," Mabel said, "since I got rid of everything from the shop. Had most of it hauled to the junkyard. And I told Jordan I'd pay him for doing some work around the house."

Lily glanced back inside. Gone were even the strips of flypaper with forty-year-old fly corpses and the box full of dentures.

Lily remembered the short bottle of sherry her mother had given her at the vineyard, and she went to the car for it. When she returned to the side of the house, she stepped up on the windowsill, holding on to the rain pipe. Mabel held out her hand and helped her up to the porch roof. "Pretty ring," Mabel said, flipping open the top, knowing the secrets of its compartment. Mabel touched her fingertip to the bit of desert dust that had collected inside. Then she released the butterfly. "In honor of the wedding of my sister," she said. And it set off in a swag, unexpectedly quick, off past the felled tree turned nearly to stone in the pasture, over the creek of rock and sand and the sagging bridge of the gravel road.

Lily showed Mabel the clear bottle without a label, marked only NO. 139 across the glass with a black grease pencil. The peachy liquid inside looked as thick as pancake syrup, and Mabel blinked and covered her eyes when the wine caught the glare of sun. "We don't have a corkscrew anymore," Mabel said.

"Doesn't matter," Lily said, and she reached into the bedroom window for the end of the heavy curtain. She wrapped the curtain around the bottle and smacked it against the house, like christening a ship, again and again, until the cork poked out a bit from the lip of the bottle. She pushed the cork out the rest of the way with her thumbs and handed the bottle to Mabel.

"It's not even nearly noon," Mabel said, taking a drink, then handing the bottle back.

"That's okay," Lily said. "It's just a dessert wine."

They passed the wine back and forth and looked off across the land. Lily thought she could see her matrimonial butterfly and its dotted-line path as it flew above the neighbor's field of cut straw and toward the condemned grain elevator at the edge of town. Lily and Mabel drank much of the wine quickly, and Lily, though not drunk, could feel the warmth of the wine at her temples and in her throat.

"Is this wine from the nuns?" Mabel said.

"Yes," Lily said, and she decided she'd never tell Mabel what their wicked stepsister had said. For Mabel, the suicide could stay the act of a lone gunman, with no witnesses. "I think Mom would've liked you better," Lily said. "You're more quiet. And you don't cuss so much."

"I cuss a lot," Mabel said.

"Not really," Lily said.

"Yeah," Mabel said. "I sure do. I'm a real salty bastard." Lily and Mabel both giggled, linking arms like old-lady confidantes.

"I called her a piece-of-shit cunt," Lily confessed in a whisper, and Mabel's wide-mouth shock and shriek of laughter was so satisfying to Lily that she leaned over and bit Mabel lightly on the shoulder.

"I could help you get the shop back together, Mabel," Lily said.

"I don't think you'd make such a great antiques salesman," Mabel said. "You couldn't sell snatch on a navy ship." Lily could not believe how funny that was, and she fell forward to bury her laughter and gasps into Mabel's stomach. The bottle fell from their hands, rolling down the slope of the roof. Lily and Mabel grabbed for the bottle, crawling quickly to the edge to see it drop to the ground, amazingly, without spilling a drop. The bottle landed with a thump without breaking, the little bit of sherry just an inch from the lip. Leaning over the edge beside Mabel, Lily felt the spin of vertigo, the clouds dipping and lifting in her sight. She still laughed as she grabbed hold of Mabel's arm, steadying herself. She felt as if the house was tipping slowly forward to gently tumble her and her sister into the tall, soft grass gone to seed.